Shift

CHARLOTTE AGELL

Christy Ottaviano Books
HENRY HOLT AND COMPANY
NEW YORK

Henry Holt and Company, LLC
Publishers since 1866
175 Fifth Avenue
New York, New York 10010
www.HenryHoltKids.com

Library of Congress Cataloging-in-Publication Data
Agell, Charlotte.
Shift / Charlotte Agell.—1st ed.
p.   cm.
Summary: In fifteen-year-old Adrian Havoc's world, HomeState rules every
aspect of society and religious education is enforced but Adrian, refusing to
believe that the Apocalypse is at hand, goes north through the Deadlands
and joins a group of insurgents.
ISBN-13: 978-0-8050-7810-7 / ISBN-10: 0-8050-7810-X
[1. Despotism—Fiction. 2. Religion—Fiction. 3. Environmental
degradation—Fiction. 4. Insurgency—Fiction. 5. Family life—Fiction.
6. Science fiction.] I. Title.
PZ7.A2665Shi 2008 [Fic]—dc22   2007046942

First edition—2008 / Designed by Véronique Lefèvre Sweet
Printed in the United States of America on acid-free paper. ∞

1   3   5   7   9   10   8   6   4   2

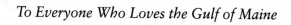

To Everyone Who Loves the Gulf of Maine

Shift

PART ONE

Destination Unknown

Mom and I have been having the same argument for so many weeks now that we've got it down cold. We can run the long version or the short version, depending on what's up, but it never really changes. It would be funny, if it wasn't boring me to death.

"Adrian, you *have* to sign up for Vacation Bible School." She usually has her arms crossed, as if that makes what she's saying more serious.

"No."

"It's a graduation requirement now. You know that."

Silence. I can say a lot by not talking.

"If you don't do it soon, it's going to be too late."

"Well, speaking of too late, Mom, how the hell does it make sense to even have graduation requirements if the world is going to end, the way they keep telling us?" I can get away with this since I know Mom thinks the Regime is way off base on this End of the World stuff. But she hates swearing.

Sigh. My mom looks old when she sighs, and I don't like that, even though I'm winning the argument.

The stalling part seems to be working. It's already almost the end of July, and I'm not signed up yet. And I won't be. The only reason I can think of to go is that maybe at Vacation Bible School I would at least meet some girls. But Daniel says those aren't the kind of girls I want to meet. He's lucky, sort of. He's Jewish so he's not required to sign up. But then again, there's a lot he can't do ever since the new Regime. Like live in my neighborhood. And that sucks.

The interesting thing about Mom's and my argument isn't so much what we're saying. It's what we're not saying:

"Adrian, if you don't sign up, it's going to make us stick out, and that won't be good. Especially for my job."

"Mom, what the heck does the Regime even need you for? It's pretty clear they don't believe in science."

And that's where I get stuck. Because Mom doesn't talk anymore. She used to tell me everything. Now I have no clue what she's doing. Working for them, I guess. But doing what? All I know is whatever it is takes her away too much, and Shriek and I get stuck here with Mitzi, the most sickeningly sweet person in Atro City. And that's another conversation we have on instant replay.

"Mom, I'm fifteen. I can take care of us without Ditzy."

"Honey"—by now she ignores the Ditzy part—"what about cooking?"

"Insta-meals. Besides, I'm good at spaghetti."

"Well, the bathrooms, then. . . . You'd never clean them."

"Shriek could do it."

"Adrian!" She gets mad because my sister's only nine and kind of on the special side.

"Okay, I'd do it."

"Be nice, Adrian. Mitzi loves you and your sister."

(Gag!)

All the arguing gets on my nerves, and the pretending is worse. Everything is not okay, and with Daniel not answering his messages (as in the last two weeks!) there isn't even anybody to complain to.

So I decide to go up in the tree.

I haven't done that for a long time, maybe years.

Dad built the fort, way back when he was still around. I was in elementary school, and Shriek had all these imaginary friends, and life was a whole lot better. I remember bringing him nails and cold beer, and how excited he was by the whole thing. It was like he was offering us nature, and there isn't exactly too much of that in Atro City. Not then, not now.

"This is the last oak," he had said, or something like that. I remember him patting it, as if he was introducing me to an old, beloved friend. Before Dad decided to make the fort, I hadn't thought much about the tree. It was big. It was there. That was about it. When I was little, I wasn't so hot on going outside since I was kind of afraid of bugs. And the rough bark was full of ants. But it was a pretty cool tree, with its wide, spreading branches. Still is. It's a miracle that it isn't dead already, considering the fact that an elevated highway runs straight through our backyard, spewing out fumes and shit.

So, I go by the garage to see if Dad's old binoculars are still hanging on the hook where he left them, and they are. I slip the leather strap around my neck and look up. The tree fort boards don't seem too rotten. I start climbing up the branches. The binoculars smash into my chest with every rung, but it feels good, like I'm finally doing something.

I think about looking for some birds, even though it's getting dark. Maybe birds are more active in the evening . . . what do I know? Dad was really into ornithology. Even the word seemed cool way back when he taught it to me, and sometimes I think I'd like to be into it, too. Just to be like him in some way. But it's kind of hard considering that there just aren't that many birds around. At least not since the Disaster. When Dad used these binoculars, it was different. There were all these little birds with cool names—like chickadee, titmouse, and jay. Hawks, even. Once Dad and I saw a cardinal. I must have been three. I remember it was the color of blood.

These days, all we get is crap birds, pigeons and gulls. They basically just want your sandwich.

I settle onto the splintery boards, hoping to see something different—a sparrow, maybe, or one with color.

Something wild.

Night arrives, and I haven't seen a single bird. So I use the binoculars to look in on Mitzi, who is dicing something for supper. Celery, probably. She's obsessed with it, because it supposedly has no calories. Her face bothers me. She looks permanently surprised from all the face-lifts she's had. I see Shriek, too, skipping back and forth in her own private world. At least she looks happy. I decide I'm not going in. I'll just stay up in the tree and look at the night sky.

That's what I really want to do, mostly because of the moon. It's going to be full, and the night is unusually clear. I'm obsessed with it. Dad's squadron is stationed there. Or was. The moon is his last known address. Five years. No messages. Nothing. He can't be up there anymore. Still, I look up and hope.

You have to hold your breath to see faraway things with binoculars, to keep the view steady. I lie on my back and stare until I'm dizzy, but who am I kidding? There's no way I'm going to see the missile silos, or guys in space suits taking a walk 250,000 miles away. The moon just hangs there, a silent white orb reminding me of Dad.

"Good night," I say to nobody, and then I fall asleep.

When I wake up, it's morning. Early, but definitely morning. Traffic honks and whines by the upper branches. I'm stiff as hell from sleeping on the boards, and I feel like a loser. (Maybe I *am* a loser.) I've got this really terrible feeling in my chest, as if I'm on the moon and out of oxygen, and it's probably just on account of all the fumes, but the feeling makes me want to do something. Only I don't know what.

That's why, instead of coming down out of the tree like a regular human being, I start climbing up. Losers do all kinds of weird and amusing things. I'd laugh, but it's me doing it. I keep climbing until I get to the branch that Shriek always called "the bridge" back when we were hanging out in the tree. It's the one that grows right over to the highway, almost like a ramp. The bridge is solid and wide. There are so many branches above me that it's easy to grab one to hold on to, and there are a whole bunch below me if I fall. Not that I'm going to fall. I'm not really all that afraid. I'm not really all that awake.

I walk out over that branch bridge and hop onto the highway as if I've been practicing this move for years. Cars and trucks whiz by so fast my pants flap. I can see the drivers looking at me, like what the hell am I doing on the highway? I figure one of them might stop for me, and I'll tell them where I'm going. I'll have to think fast, because I don't actually know.

Destination unknown.

The view from the highway is unbelievably ugly. If I were a bird, I wouldn't live here either. All I can see is city city city, in about twenty-five shades of gray. To the west, the famous Atro City chemical plants send their plumes of poison drifting into the sky. Downtown is a glittering mirage of fancy glass towers. A long line of electrical tripods, the ones that scare Shriek with all their crackling when we drive by, look like dinosaurs for some reason—and I don't care what the teachers now have to say, there *were* dinosaurs. How could anybody make up a diplodocus? The only beautiful thing is the river, a long silver poisonous snake. I cling to the guardrail. This is starting to be a way stupid idea.

Then it gets worse. A yellow HomeState copter comes buzzing out of nowhere. I duck. It's got to be illegal to be standing here on the highway. I'm just about to jump back onto the branch bridge when an ancient red car slows down, some kind of station wagon. It looks as if it's driven straight out of some old-time show starring hopeful and cheery people. They haven't made cars like this in decades. At first, I don't think there's anybody driving it, but then a little old lady leans out and yells, "Jump in!"

So I do.

"You must be out of your mind, little boy," she says. "What in heaven's name are you doing on the highway?" Either she left her face out in the rain or she's 102, but the wrinkles are reassuring somehow. Less fake, more granny-like. She frowns at me. "Where are you headed?"

"Beechmont," I say, as if I had that in mind all along. As if I have a plan. "And I'm fifteen years old." Beechmont is where Daniel lives now. Considering he's not answering messages of any kind, there's probably nobody home, and that's truly weird, since his family isn't allowed to go very many places. I'll feel better if I go and check.

"Beechmont," repeats the lady in an amused voice. "Why not?" Maybe she has nothing better to do than drive around, because she gets off at the next exit, the way you have to if you want to get to Beechmont. I'm not sure if I'm being kidnapped or humored, but for now, I'm along for the ride. "You shouldn't walk on the highway," she confides, as she does a U-turn to get onto the crosstown express. "You could get yourself arrested."

I nod and look out the window. She's right, of course. She peers at me as we screech up onto the highway again. "But I'm glad to help you, son." She pats my leg as we drive along at terrifying speeds. She tells me that her name is Myrna and all about her six cats and her four grandkids, or whatever. And it's strange how I feel safe and nervous at the same time. Not nervous because of anything she's about to do. Nervous because of what I'm about to do. By the time she lets me off, I almost wish the ride was longer. At least with her, I was going somewhere.

"Take care," she says as I hop out the door. "I hope you find what you're looking for."

Unfunny Jokes

In Daniel's neighborhood, the sun sizzles off the sidewalk. There aren't any trees in this part of town. It's hot enough to fry an egg. Almost. The time we tried it, we ended up with runny yolk on scrambled rocks, and Daniel dared me to taste it. I walk along, kicking a rock, thinking of him. Up ahead, three little girls are drawing pictures in chalk, sweat running down their necks. I smile at them. They remind me of Shriek, just in the way they're concentrating so hard. But then the rock I'm kicking skids over the sidewalk, and straight across what looks like some kind of rainbow with squiggles.

"Hey," says the biggest girl. "You kicked a rock on my angel." She points her fat finger at me.

"I saw him do it!" yells one of the other girls, standing up and glaring at me.

"On purpose!" says the third girl.

"UnBeliever!" hollers a woman sitting on a stoop. She looks like the fat girl's mom. "We don't need people like you."

"I'm sorry," I say, although I'm not. "I didn't mean to." That part is true. Then I hop off the sidewalk, attempt a meek expression, and race away. I know better than to protest. I could get turned in for actions against the government or something. I can just imagine the conversation at the HomeState office:

What do you have against angels, son?

Um, nothing?

Then why did you destroy an angel artwork?

It's better just to get the hell out of here. I round the corner and it's a relief to see Daniel's building, wedged in between the Next-to-Godliness Laundromat and Bob's Pizza. It's so familiar. I come here a lot, when I can't take Mitzi, or when I want to think aloud and have somebody answer me. The Feldsteins don't lead a glamorous life in their crappy little apartment, but they aren't afraid to talk.

"Screw your eavesdropping!" Mort Feldstein likes to yell at the wall. Maybe it's not the smartest way to be, but I admire it.

I stand outside the building for a long time, looking up at Dan's window. The blind is closed. It doesn't feel like anybody's home.

I want to leave Daniel a note, so I pound on the door. The entry to the lobby is locked. Mrs. Stickle lives in 1A—with a window right onto the front steps. She'll let me in. She's the landlady, and she sometimes brings us cookies. Lemon cookies. We joke that she's in love with Daniel's dad, but even Daniel's mom doesn't mind. That's just the way Mort Feldstein makes people feel, with his crinkly smile and his unfunny jokes. Better.

Nobody comes to the door, but I swear I see her curtain shift. I kind of feel Mrs. Stickle peeking out, so I call, "Mrs. Stickle. It's me, Adrian!"

The door clicks open and then there she is, dressed in her usual pink housecoat.

"It's me, Adrian," I say again, in case she doesn't recognize me, even though that's ridiculous. I was here a few weeks ago.

Mrs. Stickle nods at me. "Adrian," she whispers, "I'm so sorry."

What's she talking about? "I just want to go up to Daniel's for a minute. I think I left my tennis racket there." I'm lying, of course. I don't have a tennis racket. I've never played tennis in my life.

Mrs. Stickle looks at me with her old, leaky eyes, and a feeling of panic rises in my throat like vomit.

"Come in, then, just for a moment. I'll show you."

I follow her up the smelly stairs to 3B. There's

bright yellow security tape across the door: DO NOT ENTER. HOMESTATE SECURITY.

"They came," she whispers. "They came and did this." She looks around, then walks quickly down the stairs. I don't know what to do, so I just follow her. She scurries back into her apartment and looks at me from behind the half-closed door. She doesn't say anything else or invite me in. Then she shuts the door, and I know that no amount of knocking will open it again.

Constant Change

So, it had happened. HomeState had come, and Daniel's family was gone. I only hope that it might have happened in reverse order. It's possible. The Feldsteins are smart. They have friends who might warn them that it was time to go. The question is where? These were the things that Daniel and I discussed in half whispers as we practiced surviving in the desert or keeping a fire going when it was wet—all highly theoretical, since we were always in his apartment or some cement drain. But we both agreed, north was where we'd go if there was trouble. North to nature, away from the Citylands. Up where you didn't need an Identi-Card for every move.

The problem is, you'd have to cross the Deadlands.

I sit there on the stoop until I realize that the old

man in 2B is afraid to walk by me. What am I? Contaminated? Just because I know the Feldsteins? I slouch off, then start jogging. Screw it. I'm going to run all the way home.

I tear through Daniel's lousy neighborhood, past the Industrial Park zone. I'm an angry, sweaty mess, but I keep going—through the business district, with its shiny glass canyons. By now I'm walking. "Fuck you," I think at all the bankers in their fancy suits as they edge away from me.

Downtown, the crosswalks play their recorded birdsong. I used to like it when I was a kid. "Walk" is the song of the lark or something. "Stop" is a lot squawkier. It's so fake it's funny, especially for me. I know about nature and north. North's where our old cabin is. The one we haven't been to since forever, otherwise known as since before the Disaster, before Dad left, and before the Deadlands drew a wasteland on the map. Five whole years. Forever. Crazies live up there in Maine, now. That's what the official word is (which actually gives me hope, since the official word is mostly a bunch of crap). When the bombs blew, all the radiation drifted north. I was eleven when it happened. Dan and I were in his old yard. Out of nowhere, there was this huge flash up the coast. Then the ground shook like hell and the sky filled with smoke. Millions of people died, most of them in

Massachusetts. The whole country went insane, then the new Regime came to power and promised us we'd be safe as long as we Believed and wore protective gear when it rained.

North is where Daniel and I'd go.

Any other direction is for sissies.

Evening comes and I've gotten lost and unlost so many times that it's amazing that I find my way home. My feet are blistered, and I'm wheezing from so much bad air. In the chemical glow of the sunset, I see a skinny silhouette pacing angrily around our yard, stooping to snip at the bushes. Mom. She's not actually gardening—I can tell. She's waiting for me. I pick up my pace because I'm glad that she's home, even though she's going to kill me. For one thing, Mitzi's probably gone.

"Adrian," says my mother, hands on her hips, "where on earth have you been all day?"

And all night, I want to add, to rub it in. I'll bet nobody even noticed that I slept in the tree fort. But I just squeak, since I can't breathe. Mom has enough to worry about with Dad gone and her top-secret job and my sister being the way she is, but I can't help it. "Daniel's disappeared!" I blurt out. "His parents, too. Their apartment is sealed off, the way the library was . . . with all that yellow tape!" My mind races back to that day. By now Mom's leading me inside. The neighbors could be listening.

The library never opened again. Does this mean the Feldsteins aren't coming back? I just remember standing on the sidewalk as HomeState carted off the books. Truckloads. They took Mrs. Guter, too. It was awful. She was just like Daniel's dad, willing to talk about *any*thing. "And I almost got into trouble with some Believers." By now I'm rambling and Mom's saying "shh, shhh," and stroking my hair. I feel like I'm about six.

"You just can't go off like that," she says, finally, and this makes me mad.

"Why not? *You* do!"

"That's different," she says, and I can tell we're about to have another fight, which is the last thing I want. I slap at a mosquito. There's a whole battalion of them in the kitchen. They're winning the pesticide war, no question; I've never seen mosquitoes this big.

"Who says there's no such thing as evolution?" I say, swatting away and trying to get her to talk. Science stuff is usually good bait. Like, how can the government claim something doesn't exist when it's happening right under our noses? These mosquitoes are practically birds. But she doesn't rise to it; she just makes me a grilled cheese sandwich. Evolution is a forbidden concept, I know that, but she's the one who taught me about it! It's like being in a fight with someone who refuses to punch you back, not that I have a whole lot of experience in that department. I know she thinks she's protecting me. Still, I can't take it anymore.

"Good night," I say, cramming the rest of my sandwich in my mouth. Why stay up if Mom won't talk to me? She probably needs to go back into her study and run those endless secret calculations.

"Shriek's already asleep," she says, kissing me, and I tiptoe upstairs, which is ironic, since my sister snores like an old man and it would take a bomb to wake her.

I lie on my bed inventing the answers to all the questions Mom won't touch:

- Dad's not dead. He can't be dead. (Just because he can't be.)
- Mom's working on something so huge that telling me would be too dangerous. Treason. It has to do with numbers, her specialty and total passion. Codes. Codes for something big.
- Mitzi is a government spy, even if Shriek likes her and Shriek usually isn't wrong. It just makes too much sense. Mom's a scientist, and Dad is gone. We're hardly on the Model Citizens of the United Christian States list.

— Maybe even I, Adrian Orion Havoc, am
suspect. In fact, I hope I am.

Headlights roam the ceiling, swooping in crazy loops.
Since I have the window on the highway, nighttime in
my room is a light show. When I was little, I liked it,
since I was so afraid of the dark. But there are no more
monsters under my bed. It's the real stuff that scares
me now.

False Promises

I get up past noon. The house reeks of sanitizer. It's Mitzi—Queen of Clean. When I go downstairs, she's already planted in front of the telejector with her yippy little dog, Chanel, on her lap. What kind of cleaning lady comes with her own dog? The spy kind, that's my guess. She's watching a show about ice dancing. Two almost-life-size holographic skaters swish around the living room, cutting the ice so sharply I half expect frozen crystals to fly up and hit me in the face. That would be cool. Shriek's fluttering around with them, spinning and turning in her bunny slippers. I need to talk to Shriek. She might be able to tell me about Daniel, if only I can get her to think about him for a minute. She sees things that I don't. Stuff that happens far away, or is about to happen, or that happened a long time ago. But it doesn't always make sense.

I plop onto the couch and watch her twirl.

"Well, good morning to you, too," says Mitzi as Chanel growls at me. I feel like kicking him, and I'd *never* kick a dog, except that this one is basically a bad-tempered fashion accessory. How fair is it to get snarled at on your own couch?

"Your mother is at the store." Mitzi's twitchy eyes never leave the performance. "Lovely dancing, Melody," she says, clapping like a kindergarten teacher. "You're a natural." Mitzi is the only person I know who calls my sister Melody—well, except for my dad. The rest of us call her Shriek, on account of her voice. I watch as my sister attempts a triple twist, her red hair streaming out behind her as she falls.

"Hey, Adrian." She giggles, throwing her arms around me as I catch her. It's as if she hasn't seen me for years. "Where'd ya go yesterday?" That's the thing about Shriek being psychic—she doesn't know *every*thing.

"Oh, nowhere. Walking." I figure I might tell her later. I hug her back so she won't turn around and see the liposuction now being graphically carried out in our living room. Mitzi is channel scrolling, and most options aren't half as beautiful as ice dancing. "Wanna toaster waffle?" I ask Shriek.

She pirouettes into the kitchen with me as Mitzi settles into some reality show about the Deadlands, featuring twelve contestants trying to outlast each other in that nuclear wasteland. The bright colors of their survival suits contrast nicely with the swirling ash. I stand there for a minute, wondering what it would be like to try to cross over. Going through the Deadlands to Maine is the only way to avoid having to pass through New York and New Hampshire, both of which are still on fire and under fire, according to news reports. I'd take the Deadlands over roaming bands of guys with rocket launchers any day, which probably makes me a wimp.

I pour raspberry syrup onto Shriek's and my waffles. I always give her way too much. She likes to drink it off the plate.

"It's time for the midday Rapture," Mitzi commands from the living room. "Come and join me like good Christian children."

The Rapture is required viewing only once a week, and we usually skip it altogether unless Mitzi is around. Mom lets us click the "Donate Now and Be Saved" button without even watching the show, which is awful—all false promises and bad music, hymns you might hear in an elevator.

"It's that preacher with the beard," Mitzi says hopefully. "The one that looks just like Jesus."

"Great," I say, wondering how the hell she knows what Jesus looks like. Hasn't he been dead and risen and gone for millennia? "But we're going to the zoo."

And before she can find reasons to stop us, we go.

Alone Together

I like taking Shriek to the zoo. We go there a lot. She calls it the animal jail. We both agree that the animals are much smarter than most people, even if they are in jail. Shriek can watch any animal for hours, even the tortoise, and that's like watching a rock. They watch her back. When she's around, they snap out of their prisoner's identity and act almost alive, even if they are the only clones of the last existing whatever.

Like the tiger.

We always see him first, pacing his trash-strewn hill. Behind him, the signs flash DRINK COKE! CHEAP GAS! LOVE JESUS! The tiger is the black-and-white kind. He looks powerful, even though his coat is patchy with mange. Once, when Shriek looked at him, he roared.

To get to the zoo we have to take two buses or go for a very long walk. Despite the fact that it's crazy hot and spitting rain, we decide to walk. Shriek's wearing all her gear so none of the rain will hit her face and make those blisters she calls scratch. She has really sensitive skin. I'm not wearing my rainsuit. I can tell this bothers her.

"It's okay, Shriek-O," I say. "I already have zits, so what's a little scratch? Besides, you look good in plastic goggles." I'm in one of those moods where I don't care about much. I'm too busy thinking of big stuff— like Daniel. Like what Mom is up to. Like if Dad is ever coming back. Like how it might feel to actually kiss a girl.

I'm hoping Shriek might say something about this stuff—well, not the kissing—so I try leading her into it. "You know my friend Daniel . . . ?"

But she just looks blank and skips along, talking about her favorite zoo animal of all time (the penguin), and I don't want to go into any of the sad details. If she doesn't see anything, she doesn't see anything. Why make her sad? It's not her fault the world's so fucked up.

Due to my reckless mood, we end up walking through the projects. It saves time, and it's so goddamn hot that I'm not really thinking. I'm dripping sweat and out of deodorant—who'd ever want to kiss me anyway?

The projects are not very nice, and that's putting it mildly. Maybe they were, a long time ago when they were first built, but I don't know. They stick up over the elevated highways. When I was a kid, I used to think living way up in the sky like that would be nice, but the truth is the projects are pretty scary, lots of broken windows and spray-painted crap.

What's worse is the people. They're different—unhappy, says my mom, when she's feeling generous. Deranged, is more like it. Out of jobs, out of luck, out of their minds. Most of them are on drugs or huffing spray cans and have matted hair or shaved heads with beast tattoos—not exactly the sort of environment you want to take your kid sister through. And they yell. Once a whole bunch of them came after me and Daniel with baseball bats. I remember Daniel wanting to stop and try to talk to them, since that's the optimistic kind of guy he is, but I just yelled RUN, and we did.

It's nice in the projects in one way, on account of the pond. You can see birds. The pond's a drainage ditch, really, but migrating waterfowl still sometimes land there. I saw three white geese just last fall.

"Do you think we'll see them?" Shriek asks, as she always does, since this isn't the first time I've taken her through here. She's only seen people at the pond—and water rats and gulls.

"Maybe," I say, squeezing her hand. "Remember, don't look at anybody." The time before, a toothless old witch had followed us, gabbling about Shriek's pretty hair and asking for money.

"And don't talk," Shriek whispers, smiling at me.

I nod. "Pretend you're invisible." Shriek likes to pretend.

"But if I was invisible, I could do anything I wanted and nobody would see me," Shriek says, but then she clamps her hand over her mouth obediently.

It's the wrong day to walk through the projects.

There are no birds in the pond. The water level is so low that it's more like green muck, and it smells like shit. A bunch of teenagers are hanging out on the banks, drinking in plain view and pissing into the muck. I yank Shriek's hand until we're almost jogging, even though the best thing to do is *not* run, since it makes you seem afraid. HomeState never bothers to come in here. It's probably too much work for them, since the place is basically a lawless hellhole, which is why it has a certain appeal.

But not when I'm with my little sister.

"We need to get out of here, Shriek," I whisper, as I notice some guys coming toward us.

"Hey, pretty girl!" yells one of them. What a sicko.

"Faster," I hiss at her, "let's go."

We finally reach the far gate, the one that faces the zoo, and we cross the street and I can breathe. I vow to never take Shriek through the projects again. I pat the IdentiCard in my pocket, remembering my twelfth birthday and how proud I'd been to get it. Now I kind of wish I didn't have to remember it all the time, even though it does get me into places: the zoo, the mall, the gym. The library, before it closed. Those poor suckers in the projects probably don't have any cards. Who would pay the bill? Mom still pays for mine, and she's glad when I bring Shriek along since Shriek would otherwise just stay at home, dancing in circles. The truth is, I don't mind taking her places. We're kind of alone together.

"Scan and enter," says the electronic voice. "Welcome to the Atro City Zoo." Mom will be happy we aren't spending all our time at the arcade (although I recently discovered that Shriek is crazy good at WarriorPath).

The zoo's almost like nature.

Shriek beams up at me. "Mr. Baby Guy! And the lambies! Come on, Adrian, let's go!"

Silent Scream

Mr. Baby Guy is a penguin. Shriek can watch him for hours, and I have to admit, he's pretty funny. There's information on the kind of penguin he is: the rockhopper. There's this ancient video showing a whole troop of penguins merrily diving off an ice floe, then climbing back up and doing it again, like they're playing. Well, now that the polar ice cap is just about gone and Antarctica is not that icy, there are a whole bunch of floes but not that many penguins. There's only one in our zoo, in his bright blue pool in the refrigerated room dressed up in his penguin tuxedo.

"A penguin can live for fifteen to twenty years," says the recorded voice every few minutes when the loop comes round. We sit in the bleachers in the dark, watching Mr. Baby Guy do not much of anything.

I think about Dad and the moon, and start wondering if he's ever been on the dark side, the one you can't see from earth. There's so much I want to know, if I could only ask him. I blink. I'm the older brother—I've got to keep it together. But it's hard sitting here, watching that rockhopper waddle around in circles, looking like the loneliest ballroom dancer on the planet.

"Don't worry," says Shriek. "You'll be just fine." She's talking to the penguin, but I take it personally.

"Come on," I say. "Let's go see the other animals."

Outside the penguin house it's fumier than ever. Sometimes, I feel like we're breathing 99 percent exhaust, and it's almost enough to make me want a hurricane. They're scary, but they blow stuff around.

We walk through Noah's Ark Gate into the barnyard exhibit, with its pecking chickens and scrawny goats. Shriek wants to feed Harry, like she always does. Harry is her name for the old brown horse, twitching his ears against the flies.

"Why does *he* have to get burned?" she asks me, offering Harry the grass she's so carefully selected from outside his enclosure. "He didn't hurt anybody."

"What?" At first I have no clue what she's saying.

"When the End comes, Mitzi says even the horses will get their skin burned off. You know, because God doesn't like how we've been sinning." She looks up at me, her sweet blue eyes swimming with worry.

"Shriek," I sputter. This kind of stuff makes me

crazy. "Do you really think that horses sin?" This is Mitzi's fault, that's what I'm thinking. Shriek barely goes out. Thanks to Mitzi, Shriek's getting caught up in prophesies when she should be playing with her plastic unicorns. It's all those Raptures Mitzi makes her watch.

My sister pats Harry's long nose. "No," she says after a while. "They don't sin. Especially not Harry!"

"Well, then, don't think about it." This is totally lame advice for a kid who is trying to figure something out. "*Think* about it!"

"Well, when the lightning blasts us all to smithereens—"

"Jesus, Shriek!" I say as she frowns at me for using the Lord's name in vain. "Mitzi's idea of God's plan isn't what's really going to happen." There. I've said it, and I'm glad. With any luck only Harry the horse was my witness.

Shriek keeps looking at me in that trusting way of hers, so I ramble on. "I mean, who needs that much bad news? Soap operas, disasters, the forecasting network . . . you know that stuff's just made up half the time. Mitzi *likes* being afraid, but you don't have to be!"

Those telejector shows don't give you much of a break. There's always some new horror on the horizon—while Tiffany is breaking up with Brett on one channel, another channel's busy predicting high levels of radiation and a weeklong extreme heat wave. Class-seven hurricanes. A plague of cockroaches. Most of the time, whatever disaster they're talking about doesn't even happen. So why would the End be near? What makes us so Chosen?

"Forget about it," I say to Shriek. "Just use your head."

She digs into her pocket and finds some jelly beans for Harry, then solemnly holds out her little hand.

"Don't worry," I repeat, this time with conviction. "Nothing bad will happen to Harry. Believe me."

We stand there for a while, Shriek patting Harry's trusting nose, and me silently screaming. It's not fair. She shouldn't have to be thinking about any of this. I give her shoulder a squeeze. There has to be some sort of antidote to Mitzi's brainwashing besides me.

Obviously Hiding

The antidote presents itself the next day, along with a bunch of random evidence that my mom's involved in some seriously weird stuff. She's home, but acting like a visitor. Shriek's following her around, not even letting go of her hand, and this is an act of kindness, since this morning Mom was apparently so distracted that she put Shriek's hairbrush in the freezer.

"I don't like cold hair, Mom!" I woke up to Shriek's howling and my mom trying to talk to her calmly.

And the obsessive hand-holding, I recognize that. It means Mom's about to go on one of her longer trips.

"Mom, can we play Go Fish? Can we make shadow puppets?" Shriek isn't beyond working the situation a little, and who can blame her? Mom's so busy these days that she barely sits down with us. And Mom's going along with it, shuffling and dealing the cards with a blank expression in her eyes. She sits through five games of Go Fish, and she doesn't once get up to check her messages, which isn't like her at all.

So I do.

She leaves her unit running on her desk when she's home. I'm allowed to use it, which is a good thing, since Mitzi's always on the telejector in the living room. Mostly, I play games, or look at photos of when I was little, including the few we have from up at the cabin. In my favorite photo, Dad and I are sitting in our canoe, looking like we're heading out on a major voyage, which any voyage was in those days, even if we just went back and forth across the cove. We're grinning at the photographer, who was probably Mom, and smiling the exact same smile. Mom pointed that out to me recently, as if to make up for the fact that I don't have his muscles or his strong chin or really anything of his except our odd eyes: one slightly blue, one solidly brown.

Anyway, nothing is streaming across her screen—no numbers, no urgent messages flashing by—but there's a low audio going. I creep up to her desktop telejector, thinking it might be set on "conference." I don't feel like having one of her deranged government supervisors see me crawling up to the desk.

Miriam, says the disembodied voice. *Shift is*

coming. . . . Gabriel is counting on you. A white horse . . . a red horse . . . a black horse . . . a pale horse. . . . The words make no sense.

I go into the bathroom and flush the toilet so Mom will think that's where I've been, and head back to the card game.

"You're *letting* me win, Mom," Shriek whines. "Don't do that!"

Mom's obviously hiding something from us, and it's not the ace of spades.

Finally, Shriek goes to bed and Mitzi (who's still here) settles into the living room to watch a show about autopsies. I decide I have to get some answers.

"Mom, I need to talk to you." I use my sincere voice, the one with no sarcasm. And I am sincere. This is fucking serious.

We go outside into our little courtyard, where the neighbor's air-conditioning unit is grinding and the noise will drown out our conversation. It's where we talk in the summer, sometimes with lemonade. But not tonight.

Before I can start asking Mom all the things I have to know, she drops a bombshell.

"Adrian, I'm thinking of quitting the Agency." She says it like she's surprised to have said it out loud.

I nod in the dark, but I'm really shocked. She's

always worked for the Agency, before and after the new Regime, despite all the restrictions and bullshit. And these days, it's the only choice for scientists. They all have to work for the Regime. Miriam Havoc quitting science is about as weird as Mitzi swearing off makeup.

"I think this might be my last big mission," she says.

We sit there in silence. The mosquitoes find us.

"I could always teach math."

I nod again. Mom's the kind of person who can tell you the square root of almost any number, just as fast as the calculator can. She loves numbers. She says they're her way into the great mystery of creation. The saints and martyrs seem like just so much storytelling to her.

"And I'm worried about your sister."

Good, I think. At least she's noticed.

"It's just not normal for a little girl to be so intense. To not have any friends."

Well, actually, it is normal for Shriek, I think, but I don't point that out.

"I'm sending her to camp for the rest of the summer. It's this fabulous place—Stone Creek Christian Camp for Girls, way out in the western suburbs, but not anywhere near danger. I was lucky to get her in. They have horses there, Adrian. Real horses. She can learn to ride."

"Okay," I say. So that's what that strange message was about. Horse camp. Shriek will like that. But what about me? I'll be stuck here with Mitzi. No Mom. No Shriek. No Daniel. I'm about to complain, but right then, Mom puts her hand on my knee and asks, "What about *you*, Adrian? Will you be all right here alone?"

I mumble something about how *alone* would be just fine, but that I might strangle Mitzi, and Mom sort of hears me and I feel bad about complaining when there's obviously something eating her up. So I say, "No problem," and the minute I do, I know that I'm wrong.

Big problem.

True Wish

Mom drives off before I wake up. I could kick myself. I find a note by my pillow: *Don't worry, Adrian. This will all be over soon.* I can't say that these are exactly the most comforting words I've ever read.

Her note for Shriek is a bit better: *Honey, enjoy the horses! Just think, when I next see you, you can tell me all about your adventures! See you soon, love and kisses, Mom.* I especially like the part about "see you soon," even though Shriek sighs when I read the note to her (she's not exactly the best reader . . . sometimes I think all her thoughts interfere with ordinary stuff).

"Mom's so brave," she says quietly. And I nod and want to ask why, exactly, Mom is so brave, but unfortunately, I'm too afraid of what she might say. Besides,

Shriek isn't always right about everything. Once she told me that I'd have a great day at school, and I was sent to the office for laughing out loud at Mr. Darnell's ear hair (and he's the same teacher who says there's no way we're even remotely related to apes).

Shriek's leaving in a few days, too. She can't stop talking about the camp.

"You each get your own horse," she keeps telling me. "I hope mine is brown, like Harry." We look at all the Stonye Creek promotional stuff on the telejector about a million times. I have to admit, it looks nice, with meadows and snug cabins all named after the different types of horses there used to be . . . Belgian and Percheron and Mustang. I just wonder how Shriek is going to deal with all the smiling campers (the ones in the PR footage look insanely happy). I suppose it might be good for her.

She and Mitzi go shopping for a pile of riding stuff. Mitzi's great at spending Mom's money. Shriek comes home with enough to outfit an entire cabin, by the looks of it.

"E-ques-tri-an," she says joyfully. "That means for riding. And these are my jodhpurs, by the way. Riding pants!"

But the day before departure day, she clams up and stops modeling all her gear. She doesn't ask me to look at the PR stuff, or which I think is more handsome, an

Andalusian or an Appaloosa. In fact, I haven't seen her all afternoon.

But I know where to find her.

Her little toes stick out over the platform. She's in the tree fort. I start climbing. The toes disappear. Halfway up, something dings me in the head. An acorn. Then another. *Wiiing, wiiing.* The kid has good aim.

"Hey!" I yell, my voice swallowed up by traffic. "Take it easy up there."

Shriek peers over the edge and grins. "You found me."

"So, you're leaving tomorrow," I say, hoisting myself onto the platform. I know she doesn't want to talk about it, but I think maybe it's important for her to talk about it. Child psychology, or something. Nobody in our family is very good at dealing with good-bye, so I force the issue.

She crosses her eyes at me and sticks out her tongue.

"Nice tongue, Shriek-O," I say, hoping this isn't a warm-up to a tantrum. She has those sometimes, and the tree fort doesn't seem like such a great place for a meltdown.

We sit there—straight through the evening rush hour, with its sirens and stink. I'm glad she's going off to someplace where the air is better. Still, it's strangely peaceful up here, the leaves dancing in the breeze.

"Hey, a bird!" squeaks Shriek. And it is! A little

brown bird, hopping around in the high branches. "Kind of like an angel," says my sister.

"You might see birds out at that Rock Creek place," I say.

"*Stone* Creek, Adrian," she says, poking me in the belly and grinning. She stretches and slaps at the mosquitoes. Mitzi calls us from the house for dinner.

"Stay here, Shriek. Who needs overboiled broccoli? It isn't so much dinner I want to avoid as the inevitable invitation to join Mitzi in watching the evening Raptures.

Shriek shrugs. "Okay."

I know she's humoring me. After a while the calling stops.

"She's gone back to the telejector," Shriek says. "And, by the way, your feet are twice as big as mine, and I'm *starving*!"

"Me, too," I admit.

But we stay up in our tree. A mist rolls in, as orange and itchy as every evening. An early star peeks through. It winks at us, or maybe it just seems to be flickering, on account of all the smog.

"Look," I say to Shriek. "The first star . . . make a wish!"

It takes a stubborn star to be seen in these suburbs. The first star is most of the time the only star, and half the time it's a satellite. The stars always remind me of up north and our family cabin. The sky is big there. That's where I want to be. Not stuck here in Atro City. Stupid Deadlands. Stupid crazies. Stupid fucking everything.

Shriek looks at me as if she's about to tell me the secret of the universe, but all she says is, "I want there to be strawberry ice cream in the freezer." This is her true wish.

She squirms to the edge of the platform and feels for the ladder with her toes.

"Let's check," I say. It's not the first time we've skipped a Mitzi meal together and gone straight to dessert.

I have a wish, too, but it's bigger than ice cream.

There is strawberry ice cream, right between the frozen squash and the sweet peas. Mitzi has this weird habit of alphabetizing our frozen foods, and buying way too much. She thinks we have to stockpile food in anticipation of the coming of the Lord. It's just too bad she's such a terrible cook.

We sit on the kitchen floor, scooping the ice cream straight out of the carton with spoons, until the whole quart is gone. Mitzi is passed out in front of the telejector, which is playing some documentary about the vanished polar bears. A ghostly cub swims across the living room, its puppy-dog snout held high above the holographic waves.

"So," I say to Shriek. "Are you ready for this? All those horses? All that fun?"

"Yup," she says, licking her spoon.

I smile at her, pretending to be happy.

But that night, my wish grows like the worst sort of hunger until there is only the hunger and the wish, and the possibility of stars.

Half Understood

I wake up to find Shriek perched on the edge of my bed, wearing her riding helmet.

"I'm going now," she says, looking both brave and terrified.

"Yeah, horse girl," I say, smiling at her. "Have a cool time and everything."

"Uh-huh."

"And don't listen to Mitzi too much on the ride."

"Okay, Adrian," she says, squinting at me. Then she puts her face about two inches from mine. I can smell the syrup she licked off the plate. "Take care of Mr. Baby Guy," she says. "He's going to need you."

"Okey dokey." She likes it when I say corny stuff like that. I think it reminds her of Dad.

"Promise?" she says, bumping her nose into mine.

"Promise," I say, bonking her forehead gently.

It's about a four-hour drive to Stonye Creek Christian Camp for Girls. Mitzi's going to continue on to visit some friend and—hallelujah—I don't have to go. I can be trusted alone for a night.

"I love you, Shriek-O," I say, hugging her hard.

"Love you too, Adrian," she says and walks out without looking back.

Then I fall back into a strange sleep.

When I come downstairs, maybe an hour later, there are noises in the living room. At first I think they haven't left yet, but then I realize it's just the telejector— the morning Rapture on the official government station. I plop myself down on the couch, enjoying the fact that I'm not kneeling as required for the daily presidential blessing of the flag, whose broad stripes and bright stars are snapping back and forth in the holographic wind. Mitzi thinks the president is handsome, but, personally, I think he's creepy looking—the way his eyes keep shifting from side to side. He starts his presidential sermon, standing in front of people who all must be supermodels or something. They're just too perfect.

I'm about to turn it off when the president says, *"Welcome, Beloved Believers. Today's sermon will address the arrival of the four horsemen. The four horsemen of the Apocalypse."*

I shudder and think it's a good thing Shriek isn't

here. The four horsemen aren't exactly the friendliest messengers, from what I recall. I sink back into the couch and listen.

"When the Seal is opened, the first horse will appear in the heavens, a white horse. And the rider will be Christ our Lord, come to unleash the mighty power of the hereafter. This white horse will ride and conquer, and it is coming, folks. It is coming soon."

Soon. Yeah, right. The president gazes upward and flings up his arms.

"And behold, the second Seal shall be opened, and there will arrive a red horse, and it will take the peace from the earth. All the nonbelievers will kill each other. And then the third Seal, with its black horse carrying the scales of truth, shall arrive to measure the worth of the people."

As he speaks, four horses thunder through the room—a white one, a red one, a black one, and one pale as mist.

" . . . The pale horse of pestilence," the president is saying. "And Death and Hell shall follow him. And Shift shall be upon us. . . ."

And that's when I turn it off. What the hell? Shift? Colorful horses? Isn't that what the voice had said to Mom? I can't make sense of any of it. So I spend the afternoon on the couch, eating junk and playing baseball. My holographic team, with its excellent blue and gold uniforms, is beating the hell out of the team Daniel invented last summer, despite his power hitters. I play for both of us, and it's so boring that I push the brawl button over and over just to watch the players whack each other over the head and swear a blue streak. It makes a good antidote to the Raptures. Eventually I stand up and decide I have to do something with my life. Right now. Before Mitzi returns.

Shriek's voice comes back to me. "Take care of Mr. Baby Guy." And I decide that the zoo is as good a destination as any.

I avoid the projects. Strangely enough, walking alone without my sister to protect makes me less brave. Maybe courage is all just an act. I jog through the endless developments and shopping centers, following the green strip that runs under the highway, where homeless old people wilt on benches, and by the time I get to the zoo I am totally fried. I visit Harry the horse and offer him some grass that I pick from beside the fence, on behalf of Shriek. I roar at the tiger, but he doesn't roar back. I buy some peanuts, and feed them to myself. When the announcement comes over the speaker that it's fifteen minutes until closing, I have the craziest idea. I'm going to stay. Just hide out in the zoo.

The best place to hide has got to be in one of the buildings. The monkey house is out of the question—it's too smelly and too sad (the way the chimpanzees look at you with their human eyes). The reptile house is dark enough, but the snakes behind their glass freak me out. So I head over to the concrete bunker that houses the polar exhibit, with its half-dead walrus and Mr. Baby Guy, each in separate rooms. I walk up into the theater-style seats that used to be filled, back when there was a whole troupe of entertaining rockhoppers, instead of just one.

I figure there might be zookeepers, feeders and cleaners and people like that. So I lie down between the seats in the seventh row. It's not too grimy.

"Night, night," I say to Mr. Baby Guy, joking. He just stands there.

The funny thing is, I fall asleep. All that walking just about killed me.

When I wake up, I hear talking.

"Okay, Sweetie Pie," says the voice. I guess Shriek isn't the only one who makes up cutesy names for this penguin. I raise myself up on my elbows and look down. It's a girl. She's wearing a zookeeper uniform, but she doesn't look much older than me.

"Lenora's not going to let them take you," she says, dangling a fish in front of his beak. "I'll bring you some-where better. Somewhere colder." She drops the fish into Mr. Baby Guy's gullet. "Somewhere still wild."

I sit up. There isn't that much of a chance she's

going to see me, the way she's so focused on the penguin and everything. She's tall and brown and gorgeous in a not-irritating kind of way. She's the kind of girl that if I could just sit here on this sticky floor looking at her amazing hair for the rest of my life, I'd be happy. Seriously. Mr. Baby Guy likes her, too. I've never seen him this lively, not even around Shriek. He's hopping, swallowing fish, diving in his pool, popping back out. Maybe it's just the promise of food, but he's putting on quite a show. I watch Lenora adoring her penguin, and it's a nice thing to see.

She tosses him another fish. "Tonight," she says, "after they've all gone home."

This is getting interesting.

I might have found out what was going on in a more stealthy way, but just then I sneeze with a huge *kachoooooooo!* that probably wakes up the ancient walrus next door.

"Who's there?" calls Lenora, a note of panic in her voice.

I think of laying low, but it's just too ridiculous. She'd find me. Besides, she's so cute that I decide I have to talk to her. And I have something on her. I know she's plotting something. I decide to use it, the way heroes do in movies.

"Tonight what?" I ask, in my deepest possible voice, as I stride down the steps.

"Who are you?" She's looking at me as if she expected to be caught all along, but fiercely, like she's not going to say much.

"I'm Adrian," I say, hoping she thinks I'm older. People often do, on account of my height, until I open my mouth and say something stupid. "Who are you?" I don't say anything else because I can tell it would be totally brainless.

"Lenora," she says, staring at me. "I work here." She emphasizes *work,* as if to point out that she does and I don't and what the heck am I doing here after closing?

"My sister loves this penguin," I say, wanting to connect with her. She stops glaring at me and tilts her head. Her long, dark hair sweeps down over her shoulders.

"Me too," she says. "I've been his main keeper for almost a year." Her eyes sparkle, even though they're brown. I thought only blue eyes could do that.

"I like him, too," I confess, and, all of a sudden, I do like that penguin.

"Well, he's in trouble," Lenora says, wrinkling her forehead.

"Like what kind of trouble?" I ask, as manfully as possible (which means avoiding that squeaky voice thing that sometimes happens).

"Well, you know how he's old and everything?" she

asks. I nod, even though I hadn't thought about his age. "He's old, and the zoo vet says he isn't doing too well, and anyway, they're going to put him down."

"You mean, like, kill him?" I gasp.

"Yeah. Just so he doesn't die in front of some class of second-graders and ruin their day. It isn't fair."

"That sucks. That worse than sucks."

Lenora nods her head furiously. "Dr. Septic is a jerk. She's the vet. She makes mistakes all the time and says it's because she's so overworked, but guess what? I say she's just plain wrong half the time. Like about Sweetie Pie, here. He may be old, but he's doing okay. Aren't you, baby?" She looks at the bird in exactly the way I wish she'd look at me. I'd hop around in silly circles, too, the way the penguin is doing. He doesn't look like a rockhopper on his last legs. In fact, he looks furiously happy.

"So, what can we do?" I ask. I want to help. Plus, Shriek had known. *Take care of Mr. Baby Guy.* That's what she said.

"Tonight," says Lenora, "I'm taking him away."

"Away?" I repeat.

"Please don't tell anyone."

Who is there to tell?

"Where are you taking him?" It's not like she can put him on a plane back to the South Pole or something. For one thing, there's a travel ban on.

"Your bathtub?" I say, trying to get her to laugh.

"North," she says simply. "I haven't quite figured out where, but it's got to be colder."

North. That's where I want to go, but this girl must be crazy. "North? Through the Deadlands?"

"Yup," Lenora answers. "I've got a plan."

PART TWO

Calculated Risk

As it turns out, her plan involves a cooler, a bag full of squid and fish, some stolen sedatives, and a junky-looking van that once belonged to her brother Rico.

"And he was HomeState, if you know what I mean."

We're speaking in loud whispers, even though nobody else is around, and why would anyone, even the Regime, bug the penguin exhibit?

"So," she continues, "the van is outfitted with all kinds of stuff. I can cruise through the checkpoints. It will even navigate for me."

"But what about your brother? Won't he mind that you're using a HomeState van to transport a penguin through the Deadlands?"

"Nah." She shrugs. "He's in jail, anyhow. Rico's got

a drug problem. He gave the van to me before they got him."

And this sounds like the sort of thing Daniel always suspected—HomeState guys with drug problems. But I still don't get it. "You mean you'll just drive through the Deadlands and into Maine? Isn't it full of crazies?"

"Who says what's crazy?"

She's got a point there.

Within seconds, I'm telling her about our cabin and how it's right on this perfect small cove by the sea, next to mountains, and how you can see the stars.

"Okay," she says. "You can come."

And just like that, I'm in love and in deep shit at the same time.

By midnight, we've done it. It's surprisingly easy to sneak out of the main gate with the penguin. No alarms. Nobody watching. Mr. Baby Guy is full of fish and asleep in the family-size cooler. I ask Lenora to swing by my house. I figure I'll get a few things for up north, food and stuff. I can slip past Mitzi, if she's home. No problem . . . done it a million times.

As we circle down the ramp, past the top of my oak, I say, "That's my house—"

Lenora gasps and shoves my head under the dashboard. "Shit," she says. "Get down!"

"What?"

"Who's looking for you, kid?" she says in a stiff way as we shoot back up onto the highway.

"Huh?" I'm sitting up again, since her hand is off my neck. "What?"

"That HomeState car with its lights off. In your driveway."

"HomeState?" I feel like throwing up just thinking about it. "How do you know?"

"Trust me," she says. "I know."

And all these ideas run through my head.

Could it be that I forgot to hoist the flag?

Is it merely a random inspection?

Is it because I know the Feldsteins?

What if this is about Mom?

"If you're some kind of security risk, I'm letting you off," she says coolly.

"No!" I yelp. I want to go with her, and not just because she's drop-dead gorgeous. It's bigger than that. I feel like I'm *supposed* to go; it's like a Shriek feeling or something. Just knowing. It doesn't happen to me much.

"Well, toss your card, at least," she says, slowing the van. "Here—over the rail, into the projects. They can think you got mugged down there." I can tell she's serious. "Do it!"

"But I'm supposed to have it with me at all times."

— 61 —

"You choose," Lenora says. "Dump it or get out." If HomeState is looking for me, all they have to do is track the global-positioning chip embedded right under my photo.

"Okay." I pull the card from my pocket and fling it out the open window. "Done."

"That's where I'm from," Lenora says after we've driven awhile. "The projects. But I got out." Her voice sounds softer when she tells me this, not so tough. "Every time I go by, I look at Building Q to see if maybe there's another little girl looking out the window on the seventeenth floor, wishing herself away."

I don't know what to say. "You escaped" is what I come up with. I've never had a conversation with anybody from the projects, if you don't count swearing and running. And then I put my foot in my mouth, of course. "But you're so . . . smart."

She just laughs. "Except for getting stuck with you."

And it turns out she'd saved herself by going to the zoo. Her brother knew someone who knew someone who let her in for free. "So," she says, "I grew up with all the animals."

"That's funny. I bring my sister there a lot, and I don't recognize you."

"Well." She grins. "Lately I've been night shift, and before that I was the fat girl with the zits."

I blush. I have a face where zits come and go like the dandelions under the highway overpass—sometimes there are a ton of them, sometimes only one or two.

Lenora starts telling me what it was like growing up in the projects, and about all kinds of stuff. The relief of finally heading north with her beloved penguin seems to have set loose her tongue. I guess I wasn't the first person to ever think of sleeping at the zoo. She used to do it all the time.

"But never in the polar exhibit," she says, laughing at me. "The floor there is just too hard. Next time, try the snack pavilion behind the forestlands exhibit. They never lock it, and it's got a couch."

I laugh, too. "Hey," I say. "My sister would love to meet you. She likes animals way more than people."

"Sounds like my kind of girl," Lenora says, one hand on the wheel, one hand offering me some chips. I can't believe I'm sitting next to her.

And it makes me feel kind of goofy, so I ask her, "What's brown and sticky?" which is one of Daniel's dad's worst riddles. "A stick!" I yell, without waiting for her to think about it. It's so unfunny that it's funny, and that's the point. She laughs, so I go on. "Hey, a woman was driving around with a penguin, and a HomeState guy pulls her over—"

"Are you sure this is funny?" she asks.

"Yeah. Anyhow, the HomeState guy says, 'You

— 63 —

can't drive around with a penguin. You have to take him to the zoo.' So, the next day, the woman gets stopped by the same officer, and she's still driving around with a penguin, but this time, the penguin is wearing sunglasses. The HomeState guy looks at her and says, 'Weren't you supposed to take that penguin to the zoo?' And the woman goes, 'Yeah. I did. Yesterday. He loved it, so today we're going to the beach!'"

Lenora laughs for about five minutes, and so do I. We drive through the night, wedged between truckers and random vehicles, and we talk about everything: the zoo and how mismanaged it is, HomeState and how fucked up it is, and how having the Regime declare a state religion is ridiculous and unfair. I tell her about Daniel.

"What I don't get," says Lenora, "is how they think they can shove God down everyone's throat. My grandma used to read the Bible to me. Jesus is all about you and me, and not this big giant church that wants our money before it gets our souls. He wouldn't be on that Raptures show, even if they asked him. That's what I think."

And it's cool talking like this, both of us not caring what we say. I even manage to tell her about the weird message on my mom's machine, about the horses, and how Dad's on the moon, only probably not anymore, and that Shriek is at horse camp, and how she's psychic, and how I'm worried about her. I talk so much that I feel almost empty. Empty in a good way.

"Well," says Lenora, "we could swing by your sister's camp. It's not too far from here," she says, punching Stone Creek into the navigator. "You can visit. See how she is."

And that sounds just great to me.

"According to the map, there's a lake there. Mr. Baby Guy can take a bath. It's a calculated risk, but we've got to stop somewhere."

That's how we find ourselves getting off the highway about an hour later at Marshfield, where the camp is.

"Ready?" Lenora yawns.

"Ready," I say. Judging from the bonking sounds coming from the cooler, Mr. Baby Guy is, too.

Terribly Easy

The sun is climbing into a hazy pink sky. Ten minutes off the highway, we're in a different world, a world full of homes on long lawns behind fancy gates.

"Imagine the money," says Lenora.

And then there it is: the Stone Creek Christian Camp for Girls, just past the Green Acres Golf Club and the First National Church of God, with its impressive white spires. The camp sign is all chiseled stonework and ivy. And it clearly reads ACCESS BY PERMISSION ONLY.

I look at Lenora.

"Watch this," she says, pushing a button on the van's illuminated screen. The gate swings open. "Smile," she says, waving at the gatehouse, empty at this early hour. "We're on camera."

We drive straight into the camp. I recognize the Kozy Kottages from the promotional video. Nobody's up yet, which isn't surprising since it's not even six.

"How'd you do that?" I ask Lenora. "Open the gate?"

"I told ya. This used to be a HomeState van, and it has some useful features." Lenora grins, then parks by the pond. "Time for your morning swim," she says to the cooler.

I hop out and look around, wondering where the horses are. In a stable, maybe? There's a duck floating around in the pond, but it seems to be made of wood. Mr. Baby Guy waddles in to join it. We watch him swim for a few minutes.

"So," Lenora says. "Go find your sister." I'm beginning to figure out that Lenora's one of those people who gets things done.

"Ah, yeah," I say, and I want to, but how exactly am I supposed to recognize her cabin?

I barely finish my thought when a small figure in pony-print pajamas comes screeching down the path, her strawberry hair streaming out behind her like a mane.

"I knew you were here," Shriek says, all out of breath. "I dreamt you! And Mr. Baby Guy," she adds, with huge fondness. "I knew."

"Lenora," I say, "this is Shriek."

"Hi," she says to Shriek and smiles. "Would you like to feed him?" Lenora lets Shriek drop the fish into the penguin's mouth. "We're rescuing him."

"I know," Shriek says.

"Then maybe you also know that we have to get going," Lenora says. "We're taking him north, where he can live free."

"Yes." Shriek nods. "I understand." She kneels down next to Mr. Baby Guy. "Can I touch him?" she asks, holding out her hand.

"Watch out," says Lenora, as Shriek carefully pats the penguin's back. "Rockhoppers can be bad-tempered. He nips." The penguin cocks his head at my sister, his floppy crest drooping like a bad hair day. He squawks at her, but doesn't attack.

"Back in the cooler with ya," says Lenora. She lifts him up gently and puts him in. "Don't worry," she tells Shriek. "I put a little sleeping medicine in his food. He's going to want a nap any moment now."

Shriek is chewing her lip, her eyes all wide and serious. "Okay," she says, but I can tell something's wrong.

"Are you all right here?" I ask. "How are the horses?"

"They're fine." Shriek's voice is funnier than usual. "I'm fine, too." She says it so fast that I know she's covering something up. We both are.

"Well," I say, as fake and jolly as Santa. "After we take him north, I'll come right back to check on you again."

"Fine with me," says Lenora. "But here comes a chunk of attitude in a purple nightgown." She hefts the cooler back into the van, with its hand-painted Atro City Zoo logo, and points.

"Oh, no," Shriek says. "That's Brandy. She's my counselor, and she likes to yell."

"Melody Havoc," pants the counselor, her head wagging. She reminds me of my old gym teacher who used to take points off for laughing. "What on earth are you doing out of the cabin before breakfast? And who are these people?"

Lenora smiles and sticks out her hand. "I'm Nora Particle," she says, in a voice dripping with charm and grace, "assistant director of the Atro City Zoo. And this here is my trainee, who just happens to be Melody's brother."

"So pleased to meet you." I nod. "Sorry we didn't call."

"One of our specimen excursions took us right by your gates, and we decided to stop by," says Lenora.

"How'd you even get in?" asks Brandy. I can tell she's relaxing a little, like she believes us.

"We have a longstanding relationship with your camp," says Lenora so huffily that, for a second, I wonder if it's true. "Our great blue heron was found right here, on your magnificent pond."

"Oh," says Brandy. "Okay. Well, anyhow, Melody, you have to go back to the cabin."

"All right," Shriek says, throwing her arms around me.

"See you soon," I whisper, hugging her back.

Shriek scampers off as Lenora distracts the clueless counselor. "Did you know you have five species of lizard living in this pond mud?"

Brandy pales at the thought. "Lizards?" she asks.

"Oh yes," Lenora replies. "But only two kinds are toxic."

"Um, I have to get back to my cabin now," Brandy says nervously. "Nice meeting you."

Lenora smiles at me, her eyes all lit up with her bull-shitting success, as Brandy plods back down the path. "Let's get going before anybody else turns up."

We get back into the van. There's now a security guard in the gatehouse who looks at us funny, but when we smile and wave, he raises his cap and smiles back. Deception is proving terribly easy.

Easy for everyone, as it turns out. We're just merging back into highway traffic, the van programmed for Canaan—the last checkpoint before the Deadlands and home to Lenora's uncle, who's supposedly going to feed us—when a little voice announces, "I hope you don't mind, but I'm coming, too."

I turn around to find her emerging from under the messy pile of tarps.

"Shit." Lenora laughs. "Aren't you a little sneak?"

Shriek clambers into the backseat, her pajamas all grimy. "I had to do it," she says, in a tiny voice. "Horse Camp is awful. There are only two real horses and a bunch of fake ones. They're so freaky, with their staring eyes. The girls are extra mean." She chokes back a sniffle. "Plus, I'm *supposed* to come with you."

"Oh, Shriek," I say, scooping her up into my lap, "you goose." I'm sure that Lenora's going to return her to camp. Taking a kid with us through the Deadlands seems even stupider than trying to cross it by ourselves.

I look at Lenora.

"It's cool with me." Lenora shrugs, glancing at Shriek. "But you have to be smart."

"I'm smart, right?" Shriek asks, looking up at me.

"Too smart. And a little bit nuts."

"Must run in the family," Lenora says, and laughs.

And we're on our way.

Living Memory

Lenora keeps driving. She's starting to look like someone who's been up all night. I wish I could drive.

"Only an hour until my uncle's." She yawns, then pulls out of her slouch and points. "Oh. My. God. What's that?"

That is a tall mother of a mountain range of clouds. All of them dark with fury, and spinning.

"A microburst!" shouts Lenora. "Quick detour!" We speed off the exit and circle back under the overpass to ride it out. It's one sloppy storm, moving fast. Not a tornado, but loud as anything. The rain blows sideways and is full of bug parts. The whole van is a dripping mess of goop. After a while, it just stops. That's the thing about summer storms. They drop like bombs, then they're gone.

Shriek's in the back, hugging her knees. "I hope Mr. Baby Guy's okay."

"He slept through the whole thing," says Lenora gently.

I hop out to clean off the windshield. Fortunately, Lenora has some zoo-issue gloves. This goop is probably toxic, at least judging from the smell, a cross between chlorine and farts. I feel sad for a second, remembering that Dad once said a long time ago, you could drink the rain.

We get back on our way to Uncle Jack's.

"He's kind of a wacko," explains Lenora. "But he'll feed us."

Sleep is what I'm thinking about, but food would be good, too. We're running out of chips. I fall into a sweet daydream about being up at the cabin. It's a total fantasy complete with swimming, and everything being like the last time I was up there. Only with Lenora.

We pull into the driveway of a big old trailer, and Lenora gets out her cell, making me wonder for about a nanosecond if I should call Mitzi (no!).

"Hey, Uncle Jack. It's me, Lenora! Turn the telejector off. I'm in your driveway!" She's practically yelling all this, and I wonder why she doesn't just get out and knock.

"Goddammit," a voice hollers back. I see a face at the

window. Uncle Jack is a huge guy, with a lot of stubble on his face but no beard. He grins and disappears. Two seconds later, the door opens and he steps out. He's gigantic, like a football player, refrigerator size. Not only that, he's got a red and green parrot on his shoulder.

Shriek leaps out, grinning at the bird.

"Screw you," cackles the parrot. "Watch your mouth, mister!"

"*You* watch your mouth," says Uncle Jack to the bird. "Hello, Lenora, my lovely Lenora." He approaches her, arms outstretched.

"That's Ed," says Lenora, gesturing to the parrot.

"Stupidface," says Ed, nipping Uncle Jack's ear. "Buttnose."

"Excuse my welcoming committee," says Uncle Jack, reddening. "He's got a lot of bad habits. He'd talk to the president that way, Heaven forbid."

"This is Adrian," Lenora says. "And his sister, Shriek."

"Boyfriend, eh?"

"Nah," mumbles Lenora, and it's my turn to blush. "He works for the zoo, too. We're going up through the Deadlands to see if we can land a few swallowtails for a new exhibit. Shriek here's never even seen a butterfly."

Shriek's nodding along. At least that part is true. It occurs to me that Lenora is a really good liar.

"They can't fly if it isn't warm enough," says Shriek, who knows a lot about animals from all the nature programming she watches.

Lenora's uncle just stares at us, rubbing his stubble. "It ain't safe up there in Maine," he says finally, shaking his head. "That place is crawling with crazies."

"Crazies," repeats Ed. "Crazies, crazies, crazies."

"Crazier than you?" Lenora smiles, poking her uncle in the gut as the parrot ruffles its feathers.

Uncle Jack laughs but then gets all serious, his voice dropping a notch. "There are people in them woods up there." Sweat drips off his nose. "Up to no good. Hiding."

Lenora and I nod. We've heard all that stuff. Who hasn't? Shriek, thank goodness, isn't paying any attention to Uncle Jack. She's busy taming Ed just by looking at him.

"Pretty girl," says the parrot and hops over onto her shoulder.

Uncle Jack's mouth falls open. "Holy," he says. "I never seen that before. That bird is meaner than shit, pardon my French."

"Good bird," says the parrot, preening my sister's ear with great delicacy.

I'm watching all this, but at the same time I'm thinking about what Uncle Jack just said about Maine. The rumors are that after the Disaster everyone who was against the United Christian States headed north, and maybe the terrorists themselves are up there. As much as I don't like the Regime, who wants to mess with psychos? Then there's the small matter of the Deadlands. We don't have any survival suits. I'm beginning to think Lenora might be beautiful and funny, but out of her mind.

Like her uncle, except in a totally different way.

He's definitely a Believer.

He invites us inside only after Lenora suggests he might want to feed us breakfast and let us rest a bit. The inside of the trailer is all lace doilies and paintings of the saints, except for the part that's statuettes of shepherds and a whole lot of perfumey candles, lit and flickering in the middle of the day.

"Aunt Candace," whispers Lenora. "This place is like a living memory. It's as if she still lives here. She was visiting her sister in Boston when the bombs hit." Lenora disappears into the bathroom as Shriek and I sink into the couch. Ed hops from Shriek's shoulder to a fancy gold perch in the middle of the room, but he keeps tilting his head and whistling at her. She's smiling away, and this is good. Uncle Jack gets busy in the kitchenette, mixing powdered eggs and dicing peppers. Just as I'm almost asleep, he serves up a huge omelet and toast, and we eat right there on the couch. Shriek feeds some bread to the parrot.

"Ed's hungry, Ed's hungry!" he keeps insisting.

Uncle Jack turns on one of the unofficial worship channels. From across the room, Lenora rolls her eyes at me. Uncle Jack leans in close as a blonde in a bikini starts spinning a giant wheel of days.

"Jesus is coming." Uncle Jack burps. "It won't be long, and He's coming here."

"What?" asks Lenora. "Where? Here? Canaan?"

"Well," says her uncle in a wounded sort of way. "Why not? He's got to appear *some*where!"

"Like hell," squawks the parrot from his perch. "Darn tooting!"

"Maybe Thursday?" says Uncle Jack, picking something out of his teeth. "I just have this feeling. Then I can be with your aunt Candace at last."

Thursday. This man is definitely out there. Thursday is in less than a week, I think.

Not sleeping makes me lose track of time. Before I know it I *am* asleep, at least kind of, and then Lenora is waking me, saying, "Okay, well, we've got a border to cross." She's rubbing her eyes like maybe she slept, too.

She asks her uncle for some water, and he hauls out a whole case of bottles from behind a Collectible Dolls of the Second Coming set (all in their original plastic wrappers).

Handing them to me, he grunts, "You take care of her, now."

Ed barks, "Good riddance," and flies down to peck at the dirty plates.

"Thanks for the food and everything," says Shriek as Uncle Jack follows us out.

"God bless and come back by Thursday. We can greet the Lord together!"

"He's my uncle on my mom's side," says Lenora when we drive off, as if that explains it. "Just ignore everything he said."

Certain Uncertainty

We drive in silence, although there are strange sounds coming from the cooler.

"Is he hungry?" Shriek asks.

"Maybe," says Lenora. "But he's going to have to wait." I can tell she's getting tense.

We start seeing signs for Checkpoint Zero, the last security station before the Deadlands.

"I'll hide," says Shriek, suddenly. "Like Mr. Baby Guy."

"You *are* a smart girl," says Lenora. "And you, Adrian, look in that sack in the back for anything that says Atro City Zoo and put it on."

I clamber over the seat, where Shriek is wrapping herself up in a smelly tarp.

"Can you see me?" she asks, her voice all muffled.

"Nope." I tuck a corner of the plastic over her thin, freckled wrist. Then I grab a cap and a dirty fleece, both with the zoo label. Up ahead, there's an electronic billboard, the kind you see at every checkpoint, blinking its red, white, and blue message: JESUS IS COMING. ARE YOU SAVED?

"Okay, the thing to remember is, these HomeState guys are usually pretty dumb." Lenora's tone is breezy again, courageous even, the voice of someone masking fear so well that hope is contagious. Her usual voice, in fact.

She slows the van down as I grip the edge of the seat, reminding myself to breathe. We can't turn back now. There's nobody in line ahead of us. Big surprise. Who'd want to cross the Deadlands into a state full of crazies?

Lenora explains that the radiation levels this long after the bombs are low enough for us to cross, if we don't stop. "Anyway, most of the radiation blew north."

North, as in where we're going. I can't believe we're doing this.

I peek out from under the zookeeper's cap. There aren't any vehicles in the southbound lane either. That side is like a mega carwash, with hoses hanging by the wall. They must be for decontamination. The guards are all decked out in protective suits. They look like giant bugs laughing themselves to bits about us wanting to cross over, but maybe it's just the way the ventilation slits on their masks resemble hideous smiles.

The HomeState guy who comes up to Lenora's window does not look dumb. He looks mean. I can't see his eyes behind his reflective cop glasses, but I feel him studying us. Especially Lenora. He holds up his scanner, passing it once, then twice, over the van—checking for explosives and drugs. The usual. Fortunately, the scanner does not seem to have a setting for concealed penguins or little girls. And I remember Lenora said the van is outfitted with counter-devices of its own, and that we'd pop up on the list of vehicles with official clearance. So far, so good.

The guard leans into the van, his breath stinking of old cheese. "Why do you wish to enter the Deadlands?"

"Me and my assistant here, we're on a one-week official errand for the Atro City Zoo," says Lenora, not missing a beat. She holds up her badge, handing him a folder of printouts. She showed me the paperwork earlier. She's really proud of it, since she made it up herself. It looks all official, and nothing pleases HomeState more than an official seal and a big fat signature. "We're going to cross the Deadlands and enter Maine just long enough to capture some swallowtails." Her voice is convincingly calm.

The guard raises an eyebrow up over his sunglasses.

"Butterflies, officer."

He shakes his head. "You won't find any. They're all dead."

And even though I realize that he means the swallowtails, my stomach does a flip. *All dead.* I take a deep breath and think of Daniel, and how we used to prepare for an adventure like this. Only this one's real.

"Just a minute," says the guard, jolting me into the present. "Back up your vehicle, please."

My heart pounds as Lenora obliges. A second officer comes over, bigger and meaner looking than the first guy. They look at the paperwork together, talking quietly. Then the second guy uses the scanner, just the same way the first one did, but with more feeling, as if he never gets to do that and it feels good. Everything seems sort of okay until he says, "Get out of the vehicle." I start to unbuckle my seat belt, and he snaps, "Just her."

She gets out, her arms folded over her chest, her chin high, Beauty staring down the Slime. Both those guys, they're just drinking her up—I can tell even with their mirror glasses.

"I'd like to use the restroom," says Lenora, finally.

"In the building," says the supervisor, as he walks off with her.

I want to follow them, but what the hell could I do for Lenora? I'm just a scrawny kid with no skills. The first guy stands there, looking back at the building then at me, swinging his gloved hands and sort of heh-heh-hehing and smirking.

This is ridiculous. I'm going after her. Shriek will be okay since they don't even know she's with us. I open the door.

"Where do you think you're going, bozo?" booms the guard.

"Um, restroom?" My voice squeaks, but just then Lenora comes walking across the lot, the supervisor trailing her like a puppy. She's back so fast that nothing much could have happened. At least that's what I tell myself. Still, I don't like it.

When she's in the van again, the supervisor lowers his glasses and winks at her. "So long, honey," he says. "May the Lord bless. Send 'em through, Larry. Then you can break for midday Raptures and lunch." He swaggers off as I sink with relief into my seat.

The guard nods and hands Lenora a yellow card. "It's important that you read and follow these instructions," he says carefully, like someone who can't actually read too well himself. "If you have not returned within ten days, you will be reported missing. If those you leave behind can fund a rescue mission, someone may come looking. If not"—he shrugs like he doesn't give a crap—"then may the good Lord help you."

"Thanks, officer," says Lenora, as if he's just given her directions to the mall.

The massive gate swings open, and we drive into the Deadlands. I can't give a good reason for it or even believe it, but here we are.

Headed in.

"Do . . . do you pray?" I want to ask for some kind of help from someone.

"All the time," Lenora answers. "Especially back there."

And we don't say anything more for a long time.

When the checkpoint is miles behind us, Lenora turns around and says, "It's okay now, Shriek."

My sister worms her way out of the tarp onto the backseat and looks around. Just seeing her sweet little head makes me feel weird. What are we doing, driving into the Deadlands?

"It doesn't look so dead," says Shriek, and she's right. The woods and fields and empty houses remind me of Canaan.

"Just wait," says Lenora gently. "It'll change."

I turn around. My sister's eyes are wide open. I want to promise her something, *any*thing, and make it okay. But all that seems certain is uncertainty itself, so I just reach out, grab her hand, and squeeze.

Beyond Zero

It changes.

The boarded-up houses turn to melted houses, their vinyl siding sagging like burnt flesh. The green grass and the woods disappear, replaced by gray sticks and dark stubble. The gray turns to black ash, then there are no more houses or trees or sickly fields, just the swirling cinders of all that burned. An entire state and most of its people. It's inconceivable, yet here it is.

"Who *did* this?" I ask, although I've heard the stories.

"People say terrorists," Lenora mutters. "But I don't know."

"How can everyone just go on? How is watching the Raptures going to keep us safe from this happening again? How is the Regime keeping us safe? I don't get it."

"People are lemmings," says Lenora. And she explains that lemmings were these rodents that used to live way up north. Supposedly, a whole pack of them would leap off a cliff if the first one did it. Mass suicide.

"Maybe they just had bad eyesight," I say, "or got caught up in the rush."

"Exactly," says Lenora.

I read aloud from the official yellow card: "Stay alert for dense areas of photochemical smog. Avoid radioactive swamps. Under no circumstances is it permitted to exit the vehicle."

Lenora pats the dashboard. "Good van," she says. "Don't fail us now."

We ride on through a silver mist that would be lovely, except that it's fatal. Life is like that, full of contradictions. I think about oxymorons for a while—living dead, virtual reality, silent scream—until my sister interrupts my concentration with a *not* so silent scream.

"Shriek," I say, turning around. She's having one of her spells.

I hop over the seat to hold her as she shakes. And to listen. She always talks when she gets like this.

"Shift is coming." She sobs. "Oh, Mom! No." Shriek's face has gone so white that her freckles look three-dimensional. I stroke her hair. Being this way takes a lot out of her. "Mom has to give them the codes, or . . ."

"Or what, Shriek?" I ask softly. I don't want to startle her.

"Or something very bad," she says flatly, and then nods into a deep, snoring sleep. I sit there, holding her, thinking. The words "very bad" scare the shit out of me, since they can mean anything. Shriek's head flops to one side, and she drools.

"What's Shift?" I finally whisper to Lenora.

She shakes her head. "It's that stuff my uncle talks about. You know, the End of the World scenario, before Jesus comes and takes us all to Heaven. The *Big* Shift."

"The Big Shift?" I repeat. "But what exactly shifts?"

"Well, everything, basically. The earth stops rotating and whammo, everything slides over . . . the mountains, the oceans, everything. They say it's happened before, a long time ago. The north and the south poles change places or something, and you get deadly weather. It's supposed to give us sinners a chance to repent before the grand finale. Uncle Jack probably believes in it, but then again, he's a major lunatic." Lenora glances at me sideways, and I'm glad to see she's grinning. "They just want us stockpiling stuff and building Shift shelters. The End of the World is good for the economy. The people in power win again. What else is new?"

I nod. So, Shift is just one of those conspiracy theories, and they're a dime a dozen . . . like how there's a race of aliens living deep underground and controlling us all and how there's a planet exactly like earth on exactly the opposite side of the sun (where everyone has a mirror twin) and how eating more than one ChickenQuick meal a week makes guys impotent. They're out there. But why haven't I heard of it? Why hasn't Mom mentioned Shift? She lets herself poke fun at the stupidest things the Regime says and does, and this has to be one of them. Then I remember that she hasn't talked about her work in months. And it dawns on me that she's being forced into whatever plot they have going, this Shift stuff, and *that's* what Shriek is talking about. But how can Mom be involved in making the mountains slide or the poles change places?

None of it makes sense. And those horsemen. They belong to the End of the World, and that's what the Regime is predicting. . . . It all starts to become frighteningly unclear.

Shriek groans and half wakes and sits up. "We're going to save her, right?"

"Of course," I say, patting her arm. "Definitely." I'm the big brother. What else can I say?

"We're on it, sweetheart," says Lenora, and just being in it together feels better.

Shriek wriggles out from under my arm. "I think Mr. Baby Guy's awake," she says in her regular voice. "He probably needs to get out."

I need out, too. I have to go so bad I'm crossing my legs. I tap Lenora on the shoulder. "Um, I gotta pee."

She shakes her head. "No way. Not here."

Looking out the window, I see what she means.

"Maybe we can just let him out inside the van?" says Shriek, all her attention on the cooler.

Surprisingly, Lenora agrees. She doesn't want her baby suffering, either. "He bites when he's mad," she says. "So be very careful lifting him out."

But this is Shriek we're talking about. She'll be fine.

"Good morning," says Shriek as she undoes the lid, even though it's midafternoon. "You can come out now."

But Mr. Baby Guy just *skeek skeek skeek*s his discontent, making Shriek giggle and filling me with bizarre relief. The world is lost and gray, but there's laughter in it, and the smell of penguin shit. Life will go on, and maybe even get better, even here in Hell.

Living Eternity

It's a living eternity before we start noticing signs of life. First Shriek sees a bird winging its way east to the sea. Then the landscape changes. It's no longer completely flat. The gray rises up and becomes the outline of trees and then houses. By the side of the road, there's a shoot of green. It sticks up out of the ash like the most beautiful thing on the planet, but I have to pee so bad it's hard to take anything in. I grimace at Lenora, who grins at me, then says, "Okay, you can. In a few miles. But the penguin stays in."

By now, Mr. Baby Guy is out of the cooler and crapping all over the van, making those cute noises and keeping Shriek entertained.

By the time Lenora pulls over, we're seeing trees. Trees with leaves. Their branches tangle up in each other, not daring to reach for the untrustworthy sky. Jumping out, I try to avoid the drifting ash, which must be radioactive. Lenora was explaining it to me: the Deadlands are going to be dead for a long, long time. I race behind the van and steam a big pisshole in the thick dust of doom, then I hop back on board, feeling much better.

The scenery is getting better, too, reviving itself in front of our eyes. We're far from where the bombs fell, now—probably almost to Maine. And I'm so afraid of what we'll find there.

"It's just too fucking bad the clouds all blew north," says Lenora, reading my mind. "And all that radiation rained down. Or this would be a paradise. . . ." She sighs as we cross over the bridge. I know where we are now. It's the bridge with the sign that says WELCOME TO MAINE—THE WAY LIFE SHOULD BE, only the sign's gone now and the bridge is empty and unpainted.

"Listen," Lenora says, pulling over and collapsing dramatically on the steering wheel. "I'm totally fried. I don't think we should stop here, but I can't drive anymore. How about you?"

I nod, sure thing, but really I'm scared to death. The only time I've driven is in telejector simulation, featuring outrageously high speeds and tons of wreckage.

"But Adrian," Shriek reminds me, "you don't know how to drive."

This doesn't seem to matter to Lenora, who has left the van running and crawled way back into the tarps. She's asleep within moments, one arm over her face. I slide into the driver's seat, and Shriek hops up front. I put my foot on the accelerator and we lurch down the road.

Driving's not that hard, actually. Especially when there's no traffic. Not one single car. I have to stop myself from driving way too fast. But it almost doesn't matter. There's no sign of anybody at all, in any of the plazas or houses we see from the highway. I just keep driving, hoping this is the right way. The last time through, I was a kid. All I cared about was where to stop for onion rings and lobster rolls, not how we actually got to the cabin. At the mere thought of fried food, my stomach growls. It's been ages since Uncle Jack's. In fact, it must be dinnertime. But every single gas station and snack spot we pass is deserted. Pete's Pancake House. Closed. Miss B's Diner. Vacant. Ike's Ice Cream—49 Flavors! Boarded up. I resort to sucking the last strings of fake cheddar out of the Cheesi-O can, one hand on the wheel like a pro. Maybe it's because we're finally out of the Deadlands, maybe it's because driving for the first time is so cool, but for whatever reason, I'm full of optimism.

Shriek puts down her window and leans out like a puppy. The sky is blue. True blue. No chemical haze, no factory fog. Some of the worst poisons are invisible—I know that. But still, the deep, clean color pumps hope through my heart. I hear Shriek take a good, long whiff.

"Flowers," she says. "It smells like flowers."

I drive and drive until it's pretty clear we're having a penguin emergency. Somehow, Lenora can sleep through it. But when even Shriek can't calm Mr. Baby Guy down, I pull off the highway toward a sparkling bay. There's nothing in the harbor but sunken sailboats. Their masts stick up out of the water like some kind of weird forest. By now, Lenora is awake since I'm actually not all that great at taking corners. Or stopping, as it turns out. We screech to a halt and spill out of the stinking van. Stumbling around, we blink at the last bit of day. The penguin waddles around in hyper circles.

Then Shriek screams.

She's pointing straight into the setting sun. I can't see anything at first. Something is dangling out over the water. It looks like one of those rope swings, the kind I was always too scared to try up at the cove when I was a kid. Someone seems to be on it, swinging gently back and forth, not daring to jump. I shield my eyes from the glare as Shriek hides her face in my jeans. The person isn't a person, not anymore. It's a skeleton with shredded clothes, a corpse! Lenora gasps. She chases down Mr. Baby Guy and carries him back into the van like a football. I hoist a shaking Shriek into her seat and will myself to look away.

"We're outta here," Lenora yells, back in the driver's seat. "What the fuck?"

All the rumors come back to me. *There's nothing but zombies up there. Mutants. Godless imbeciles. We ought to just erase it from the map.*

The sky is still blue, but everything is wrong. "Just keep driving," I say, making my mouth form words. "It will be okay up at the cove."

"You're just saying that," Shriek says, and I can tell she's about to wig out. "That doesn't make it true."

"No," says Lenora. "But it helps."

Blissful Ignorance

We drive in silence and very fast. Mr. Baby Guy manages to jump onto the seat next to Shriek. She belts him in. He looks confused and ridiculous. The van smells like the zoo on a really bad day. The sky, now full of puffy postcard clouds, is so beautiful that it's practically painful, but I can't trust it.

"How far?" asks Lenora.

I look at her. "How should I know? What about the van navigator?"

"Not working," she says.

"You're kidding."

"Nope."

"Okay." I guess. "Three hours." That seems about right.

"Okay," she echoes back. "We'll drive until we're out of fuel."

Out of fuel? "And then what?"

"Then we stay."

"You mean, like, not go back?"

Lenora doesn't answer, but Shriek does.

"We're not going back, Adrian."

I'm an idiot. I feel like the girls know something I don't know, and if this is blissful ignorance, then I don't like it. I'd rather *know*. "What do you mean?"

"Well," says Shriek, "all I know is we don't go back."

"And all I know," Lenora says, "is in seventy-two miles we'll be out of gas."

I'm staring at Lenora. She must have suspected all along that we'd be stranded up here. I don't want to overreact, but what the hell?

She pulls over and shrugs and gives me a smile that goes a long way to making me feel okay, but only if I don't think about it too hard. Stuck in Maine with the woods full of crazies and my innocent little sister.

"I think Mom and Dad are here, too," Shriek says, and I roll my eyes until I realize that me being such a grouch isn't exactly going to help anything. I turn around and smile at her.

"Sure," I say. "Why not?" I don't mention the 452 reasons that come instantly to mind. . . .

We drive until we have to get out again. The sky is pink with clouds, and the green smell of the pines is stronger than air freshener. We're just about to get back in and keep driving, since this isn't the sort of place to release a penguin, when a woman's voice startles us.

"Atro City Zoo, eh? You've come a long way."

She traces the letters of the logo on the side of the van with her long fingers. I want to warn her that the dust is probably radioactive, but instead I just stare. Where did she come from? She's wearing a dress covered in stars, something like Daniel's mom would wear, and her feet are bare and strong-looking. No toenail polish, just plain old toes. I can't take my eyes off her.

"We've got to get going," Lenora says, her voice all edgy.

"Of course you do," says the woman. "But first you must visit us. You look hungry."

My stomach's so empty it's practically inside out, but I try not to nod too hard.

"My name is Grace Ellen," she explains. "You will be our guests." Then she walks straight off the highway, into the woods, glancing back over her shoulder every so often, like a mom. She's one of those women whose age is impossible to tell. Her smile is young, but her eyes are old, or maybe it's the other way around. "We don't get too many guests anymore, as you can imagine."

We follow her, Shriek skipping down the forest path in her dirty pajamas, Mr. Baby Guy hopping slowly after her like a miniature drunken boyfriend. Rockhoppers are definitely not creatures of the forest. Finally,

Shriek leans over and scoops him up. Mr. Baby Guy shakes his head back and forth and lets out a long *skeeeeeeeek,* but puts up with being a penguin teddy bear.

"Stop that," says Shriek, firmly, as the penguin wriggles in her arms. "No nipping!"

I take Lenora's hand—I'm not sure why. I'm too tired to care what she'll think, and the thing of it is, she doesn't let go. So we walk through the sunset woods holding hands. It's a sweet path, lots of moss and pine trees. Tiny ponds the color of tea. Perfect for hand-holding.

"It's just like I pictured it," says Lenora, in a dreamy voice. "All these trees." We're walking slowly, and Lenora keeps bending down to smell stuff, to look at leaves and rocks up close. She seems to be memorizing the landscape, in case she never sees it again. "It's *so* beautiful—just the earth being the earth, without all the shit we've done to it."

Yes, and there are probably mutant wolves about ten feet away and bears, and nuclear fallout all over the damn place, I want to add, but I don't. Because she's right. It is so calm and lovely, and we're holding hands, and I can't seem to speak.

World's End

The path ends in a clearing in the wood, where a small shingled house hides behind real roses. Shriek and Mr. Baby Guy are inspecting a garden full of flowers taller than they are. A few are even taller than I am! Yellow flowers with big blooms, like bent-over shower heads . . . and a whole bunch of chickens scratching at the dirt. Mr. Baby Guy's cocking his head and looking annoyed, probably wondering where the squid is.

"Are these sunflowers?" Lenora asks. "I've always wanted to see sunflowers." She reaches up and pulls a giant bloom to her face, leaving my hand feeling both empty and full. Full of having held hers. As Lenora studies the flowers, I study her. I'll bet she hasn't seen much nature, an Atro City girl from the projects like her. Maybe she's visited her uncle in the trailer—there were trees there and everything, but nothing like this. "I've never seen a garden except my grandma's potted tomatoes," she says, and the wonder shines in her eyes.

"Welcome to the End of the World," says Grace Ellen, smiling, "where we grow what we need and the earth provides."

"But . . . isn't it unsafe?" I blurt out. "With all the radiation?" I feel stupid bringing this up.

"Yes, we have suffered," Grace Ellen answers calmly, gesturing at the pots of lettuce, the soft red tomatoes, the dark green whatever-it-is. "I am healing the garden, and the garden is healing me, and time will heal all of us. Come in. You must eat."

Eat. I like that idea.

The three of us follow her, leaving Mr. Baby Guy outside, surrounded by the pecking chickens. He just stands there stiffly, a puzzled king towering over his squawking subjects.

The inside of the house is warm and dark. It takes a moment for me to see anything. Most of the room is taken up by a huge frame with strings, a loom, says Grace Ellen, when Lenora runs her fingers over it. It's for making cloth. Out of what, I wonder. This place is a fairy tale: no telejector, no micro. Just furniture and a huge black woodstove pumping out heat on a summer's day. I know about woodstoves. We've got one in the cabin. They're great when the power goes out; you can cook on them in an emergency. Grace Ellen is definitely baking something that's making my mouth water. I take a deep breath and smile with relief. The smell of baking bread just seems to guarantee that there is no evil here. Bad guys don't bake bread. That's what I want to believe, as I look around. A small black cat presses itself against my shins, then weaves back and forth between Shriek's little legs, purring its heart out.

"Midnight," Grace Ellen says. "She lives here, too." She gestures at a large, low couch. "Sit, sit, and I will serve you."

We collapse on the soft couch, under a wall full of bundles of dry herbs, drying in the heat. The whole place smells like a garden mixed with that baking fragrance. My body start to relax for the first time in days.

Grace Ellen brings us bread. The crust is crisp, the inside is soft, and there are tomatoes and cheese. That's all, but it's the best feast ever.

"From my goats," Grace Ellen says, pointing to the cheese, and I guess I didn't even know that goats gave milk. I've never really thought about goats, except for the grungy one in the zoo with his weird horizontal pupils. Maybe all goat eyes are like that.

"Goats?" asks Shriek, bouncing out of the couch. "Where?"

"Tethered in the far field," says Grace Ellen, "by the river. If I let them stay around here, they chew everything in sight and swallow half of it."

When we finish eating, I slouch back into the couch and look around. It's only then that I realize we're not alone. A tiny old woman sleeps in a rocker in a shadowy corner behind the stove. Her hands flutter, and her eyes pop open. Instantly, those eyes are on me, watery and pale. I look at her and it's as if I'm seeing through her eyes, into someplace beyond. I look away, shivering despite the heat.

"Black rain, falling ash," calls the old lady, waving merrily at us. "So, you have run, too?" She's swinging her feet now, feet that don't reach the ground. The rocker kicks into action.

"Hush, Veronica," Grace Ellen murmurs. "Would you like your afternoon tea?"

"We have seen death," the old lady hoots, "but we are still alive."

"You'll frighten them, dear," Grace Ellen responds. "Stop it."

"All the birds have flown," cackles the tiny lady, who isn't listening at all.

"Oh, don't mind Veronica," Grace Ellen says, tucking her loose hair behind her ears. "She's one of the

Deadlands survivors. She's seen too much. And just the other day, I saw an entire flock of starlings. I am sure of it." She puts her hand on my shoulder and stares at me for a long moment. "Your eyes," she says. "There was a man here just after the Disaster. He had your eyes. You were meant to come here, too."

"What was his name?" I ask, my heart picking up speed. "The man with the eyes?"

"He didn't say," Grace Ellen says, folding her arms around her slight body. "So few people do, these days." I get the feeling that there's more to tell, and that she won't tell it. Instead, she bends over and touches Shriek on the shoulder. "How's the cheese?"

"Good," says my sister, her mouth full. The old lady is beckoning at Shriek to come over. My sister looks at me and I shrug. Slowly and politely, she creeps up to the rocker, the way someone might approach a jumpy dog or perhaps a queen. In a flash, the old witch snatches up my sister's hand and presses it to her scrawny breast. Shriek pulls her hand away and looks at me.

"The world will end, over and over," mutters the lady. "They say we will see paradise in the afterlife, but paradise was once here. Then the bombs and the fire. All the burned bodies. All the burned children. . . ." Her empty eyes suck in Shriek as if she's the last child on the planet. This is as bad as any sermon on the telejector. I hop off the couch and yank my sister away.

"Veronica," scolds Grace Ellen quietly. "You are upset. Let us say a calming prayer."

Great—a prayer. How totally useful. I'm ready to march us all out of there, despite the bread and the soft couch. But instead I find myself holding Veronica's clawlike hand as she stays in the rocker, and Lenora's hand, too (this I can take). Grace Ellen has just fed us, so I figure it's only polite to listen, even though praying out loud gets on my nerves. It always seems like showing off. Can't God just listen to us think? But everyone is doing it, so I bow my head. I'm tuning it out the way I always do, when I realize that Grace Ellen is saying unusual words—

> *Eternal Spirit,*
> *Earth-maker, Pain-bearer, Life-giver,*
> *Source of all that is and that shall be,*
> *Father and Mother of us all,*

God isn't just an old man in the sky? I decide this might be worth listening to.

> *Loving God, in whom is heaven:*
> *The hallowing of your name echo through*
> * the universe,*

The way of your justice be followed by all
the peoples of the world.

I look up at Grace Ellen. Her eyes flicker open and smile at me, even though she seems completely engrossed in what she's saying. All peoples of the world? This is truly different.

Your heavenly will be done by all created
beings,
Your commonwealth of peace and freedom
Sustain our hope and come on earth.
With the bread that we need for today,
feed us.
In the hurts we absorb from one another,
forgive us.
In times of temptation and test, strengthen
us.
From trials too great for us to endure,
spare us.
From the grip of all that is evil, free us.
For you reign in glory of the power that
is love,
For now and for ever.
Amen

I actually say amen, too.
I almost want to hear the whole thing again.

We let our hands fall to our sides in that circle, and I feel something. It's more than the burning urge to kiss Lenora, although I definitely feel that. . . . Her hand is warm, and I'm still holding it. I wonder if it's okay to think about sex and religion in one breath like this, or if I am just some evil, polluted kid. Standing in this strange circle, I don't think so, somehow.

God is bigger than that.

Minor Miracle

We leave Grace Ellen, each with our own regrets—Lenora that she can't stay and work in the garden, Shriek that she didn't get to see the goats, and me that the hand-holding stopped.

"You are always welcome," says Grace Ellen, standing in her doorway, Midnight the cat slinking in and out, old Veronica hollering prophesies from the dark inside. "I don't go anywhere anymore," Grace Ellen adds, pointing at an old car claimed by vines and rust, "so people must come to me."

And I do hope we come back someday, I really do, but right now we have to go. It's getting late, and I don't want us on the road when it's dark, in case I have to start trying to recognize landmarks or something.

Now that we've been away from it, the van smells extra bad, and we perform a minor miracle, all three of us, with rags and twigs, scraping off the worst of the fishy penguin crap. Mr. Baby Guy prances around, no doubt planning to shit it up again. But we're in okay moods, considering everything. In fact, Shriek is singing to herself, the way she does when she's happy.

"So," says Lenora, "let's get this penguin back in his cooler and up to that cove of yours."

I nod. I like the way she says "cove of yours." I want to be the one to show her everything—the mountains, the blueberry fields, the sea. It's not too far now, it can't be.

As we drive off, Shriek lies in the back singing a tuneless song about butterflies. "You know, Adrian," Lenora looks at me and says, "sometimes I think heaven is right here. Not later. Now. Heaven."

And with the sky wide open, and the forest green, I know what she means.

"Hell, too," she adds.

"Definitely." I just feel like agreeing with her.

"I'm in awe of the universe." Lenora grins, completely unaware of what her smile is doing to me. "Our thoughts matter, Adrian. God wants us to think."

Well, I know what *I'm* thinking, and I hope God doesn't mind. She's just so beautiful—Lenora, that is—but maybe God, too. Who says God has to be an angry old man with a beard?

"You mean, like a scientist?" Mom always insists

that the scientific basis of reality is so strange that it gives her shivers and keeps her up at night contemplating the stars, our cells, the universe. . . .

"Yeah," Lenora says. "Or an artist, or just a regular person. Anybody who uses their mind, because mind and matter are one. . . . That's it, that's God. One."

She's lost me there, but I nod.

"We can create our destiny," she adds. "For example, me wanting to rescue our penguin. I planned it and thought it out, but then I had to leave stuff to chance— and *you* showed up. Like a gift."

A gift. My cheeks burn. I feel like kissing her, but she's driving and Shriek's watching, so I just say yeah, in this totally lame voice. But somehow I don't care about being lame in front of her. Because I see what she means, sort of. The things that don't make sense are the *only* things that make sense.

We keep driving but stop talking, and all of us are thinking really hard. I can just tell. This is a voyage to something big, that's all I know. The sun is low in the sky when we find Coastal Route 1, which I pretend to remember. The navigator still isn't working, so it's all guesswork from here on in. We go through towns flickering with ghostly light, shreds of old laundry still hanging on the line. I'm so tired that I sleep a bit, and in my dream Shriek is telling Lenora where to go.

"Turn left by that Dumpster," says my sister, and I wake. The dark shape of the Dumpster in the tangled bushes looks just like where Mom and I once saw a bear near our cabin by the cove.

And it is.

We come down over the final hill, and the sea spreads out before us. The road follows the edge of the cove, and the sunset mirrors itself in the water, all pink and blue. We drive by a few other cabins, then the row of mailboxes, then there is the woodshed, its roof sunken in and its walls sagging. A memory of Dad comes to me—he's chopping logs in half with just one swing of the ax. "Wood warms twice," he always used to say, sweating as he worked. And there is our cabin itself . . . with smoke rising out of the chimney.

All the talk about zombies and godless imbeciles comes back to me in a single bolt of fear. "Keep driving!" I gulp, too panicked to even want to peek.

"All right." Lenora shrugs. "But we have to get this little guy into the water."

We follow the shore road until the old bridge and pull over. Across the cove, I see our cabin. I smell the smoke. Someone's in our cabin and it's not us. It's not fair.

The girls don't seem to care. All they're thinking about is the penguin.

"Okay, Mr. Baby Guy," says Shriek quietly, "it's time."

Random Logic

It's almost dark when we stumble our way down to the patch of rocky beach under the bridge. Stars twinkle in the sky and in the sea.

"Like falling diamonds," says Shriek, poking at the water with a stick.

Lenora lifts Mr. Baby Guy out of the cooler with extra care. She strokes his silly yellow crest.

"*Skeek skeek skeek*," says the penguin. His red eyes shine in the night.

"Mr. Baby Guy," says Shriek, on her knees. "It's okay to swim away now."

"Hey, Sweetie Pie," says Lenora. It sounds like she's holding back tears. "Go on."

But Mr. Baby Guy is not interested in the water. Maybe he's never seen waves before, and they scare him. Maybe he realizes that he's nowhere near the South Pole—in fact that he's in the wrong hemisphere entirely. He hops loudly around on the rocks (there's a reason his kind are called rockhoppers), *skeek*ing crazily and tugging at the long grass.

"Is he trying to build a nest?" I wonder, remembering the educational video at the zoo, and how rockhoppers line their nests with grass. I must have seen that loop about ninety-five times. Nowhere did it mention penguins in Maine, or even anywhere up north. Maybe this wasn't exactly the most brilliant idea.

"I don't want to force him." Lenora sighs. "It's better if he finds the ocean for himself."

I can tell that this is really hard for her, and I do care, but mostly I am thinking about the cabin.

"Will there be sharks?" Shriek worries aloud, but nobody answers her. We're all getting cold and cranky. I keep looking at the smoke rising from my family's chimney. There's a light now, too, behind pulled curtains. I remember those curtains. They have these small embroidered holes in them, not that you can tell from here.

Clouds blow in and hide the stars, and all of a sudden, it's freezing.

"I'm kind of glad about the clouds," confesses Lenora, looking up. "It's way too big out here. It makes me feel tiny." She's hugging the shivering Shriek, whose pajamas are thin as paper. We hang around, waiting for Mr. Baby Guy to swim off to freedom, until I'm so tired and frozen I decide to go sleep in the van. The girls stay, though, to watch the penguin liberation.

"Okay," I say, wrapping Shriek in my Atro City Zoo fleece. It's so quiet that you can hear the slap of each wave tumbling the pebbles up and down the beach. "Someday, all of these stones will be sand." The thought just comes to me as I skip a flat one off into the watery void. Lenora looks at me as if I've said something profound. I shrug manfully and kiss them both good night. It just seems like the thing to do. I take the warm feeling of Lenora's lips to sleep with me and dream of so much more.

When I wake, it's that gray time right before dawn. The moon is setting over the mountain. "Hey, Dad!" I say, out of habit. "We're here, up at the cabin!" I think he'd like that idea, even if we're not exactly *at* the cabin.

Lenora and Shriek are curled into each other in a crevice in the rocks, both asleep. Mr. Baby Guy is nowhere in sight. I scan the blank water. "Farewell," I whisper, and feel sad and happy at the same time. With our penguin mission accomplished and someone living in the cabin, I feel stuck. And there's that stuff about Shift. It's probably just more Mitzi crap, but I can't stop thinking about it. I decide to go for a walk before the girls wake up, just to clear out my brain.

I don't dare walk toward the cabin. Instead, I head off down the far side of the cove to the place where my dad and I once spent a day building what he called cairns—big piles of stones. They were for marking a path or remembering the dead, neither of which we were doing on that day all those years ago. Where I remember them being, there's nothing much—just rubble—so I get to work. It's satisfying for some reason, hauling big rocks and piling them on top of each other. My cairn's pretty tall when I realize that the sun is climbing. I need to get back. I'm hungry enough to eat seaweed, which is edible, I think, not that I've tried it. That's got to be our next move, I realize: finding food.

I race off to where we left the van, to where the girls were sleeping. No van, no girls. What? I choke out their names, "Lenora! Shriek!" Whitecaps are forming out at sea—the wind takes my voice away. They wouldn't just leave me! Someone must have come for them.

The crazies . . . who else?

I stand there paralyzed by fear, but just then a wasp zings by. I can see its stinger—it must be the size of a sewing needle. This is one mutant monster wasp. I don't stand still, the way Dad taught me to do with regular wasps. I run, fast and without thinking, home to my cabin.

There, in plain view on the deck, is a man. A crazy guy, his wild hair flying and his arms flapping all around, his face turned up to the sky. What if he looks my way? I do an about-face and run like hell, past my stupid cairn, until my legs hurt and I have to walk. I make it to the far end of the cove, where the pine tree point juts out into the sea. It's not someplace I've ever come before. The wind rustles around in the woods like it's looking for me, too. There are twitterings and crunchings in the bushes.

I'm screwed.

Over the mountains, dark haze gathers. A black air-craft floats silently by the tallest peak. I hold my breath. It's either HomeState or terrorists, and I don't know which is worse.

I collapse on a rock, so thirsty that my tongue's stuck to the roof of my mouth. I'm tempted to drink saltwater, but that's slow suicide. Not that lying here in full view of anybody who's looking for me is all that much smarter.

I spend the afternoon hiding under some branches wondering what Daniel would do. He would . . . do something. I have to find Shriek and Lenora. Where do I start? Finally I get up and walk farther down the point. I always thought there weren't any houses at this end of the bay, but I come to an old shack in a clump of trees. It looks abandoned; it might be a place where I can hide and think. The door sticks until I lean on it, then it flies open and I fall face-first into the spidery darkness, sneezing my head off.

There's only one cupboard, but I get lucky. It's a museum of canned food—all of it coated in dust and mouse droppings, but there for the taking. Ravioli, pineapple, mushroom. Pickles, chicken noodle soup, creamed corn. A rusty can opener does the trick. Anchovies. I don't even *like* anchovies. It doesn't matter. I chug a can of ancient soda and fork food into my mouth, hardly even tasting it. I eat so much that I feel sick and there's still plenty left over for later. I go out on the rickety little deck overlooking the cove to suck in some fresh air. Now that I've eaten, I can almost think. Now that I can almost think, I feel even worse. Lenora and Shriek are gone, probably kidnapped by crazies, and I don't have a clue what to do next.

There's an old canoe wedged upside down under the deck, and I decide I'm going to paddle down-cove, to get a good look at our old cabin from the safety of the water. I've got to find out who's in there. The paddle is in the canoe, and, once I scrape out a bunch of spiderwebs and mossy crap, I push the boat over the rocks and into the sea. Cold waves slap my thighs as I wade out. I practically spill overboard getting in, but it feels good to be *doing* something. I search the cove for Mr. Baby Guy, or boats, or any sign of life, but it's just quiet. Too quiet. There's only a distant hum somewhere beyond the mountain. I head along the shore, toward our end of the cove. Paddling solo is hard. I'm not used to steering, I never did it as a kid, but I do an okay job zigzagging my way across the water. There's no smoke rising from the cabin. Maybe whoever it was is gone. I just want to go home, and the cabin is the closest thing I've got.

I'm almost there when I see them. People on the deck, at least three of them. The scraggly old guy walking in circles, flinging his arms around like he's arguing with someone, a very short person (a kid?), and an enormous black guy holding a gun. He's staring in my direction. Their voices carry over the water.

A man's voice says, "Watson, you'll (something something) the far end, right?"

"No problem. Any action there, we'll (something something) their brains out. They'll be sorry they ever (something)." This is a woman talking.

"(Something something) I'm sick of waiting any-how," a third voice joins in.

"Who's that (something) over the water?" calls the woman.

"Hey! You!"

One of them is yelling and it must be at me, but I don't know for sure. I'm paddling frantically in the other direction. The wind roars in my ears.

"Come back here, or we'll (something something)" is the last thing I hear them say. I'm almost at the little shack when I fall out of the canoe. The water is freezing. Good temperature for Mr. Baby Guy, but not me. I haul myself back on land, stash the canoe under the collapsing deck, sprint up to the shack, and sit there panting. I peel off my wet clothes and grab a jacket off a hook by the door. It's someone's old hunting jacket—plaid, red, and itchy next to my bare skin. It smells like wood smoke and ancient sweat, but I have to get warm. I think about making a fire in the leaky-looking stove, but then those people in my old cabin would find me. I'm too damn cold to care. What the hell. I'll build a fire. Lenora and Shriek are gone. If I want to survive to find them, I can't freeze to death first.

I start stuffing old newspapers into the firebox, trying to remember how to start a fire. It's not something I've ever really done. Dad always did it. Or Mom. And once I helped Daniel start one in a gutter so we could roast marshmallows. Wadding up the old newspapers, I read: *Better Armor Reduces Casualties, Woman Gives Birth to Puppies, First National Church of the*

Good Samaritan Builds Billion Dollar Cathedral, and a whole bunch of stuff from years ago. Finally, I get something going, and that something is smoke.

My eyes sting with it. I can't see the flue that I just remembered you're supposed to open! I pull on my wet jeans and run back out onto the deck. It's dark and windy, but at least I can breathe.

That's when it starts.

Bright Night

At first, it's just a whisper of color in the sky—a red shimmering, then purple, then green. The streaks grow bolder, and the colors start to pulse and dance high overhead. It's beautiful and very strange, especially when the streaks start flowing into a sort of robe, the kind Jesus might wear if he were a thousand miles tall. A roaming light comes up over the mountain, searching the sky, maybe searching for me. I'm cold down into my bones, but my shivering is all about fear. *Atone for your sins,* the sky seems to be saying, as flames lick the dark. All my life, I've heard about the Apocalypse, but it was for people like Mitzi to believe in. How could she be right? I retreat into the cabin and throw myself under the musty covers of the one little bed. I curl up into a ball and wait.

It's God's very breath blowing on the sky.

Soon, I'll probably hear His very Voice.

He is coming.

I'm not ready.

But there's no voice. Only my heart thumping, and mouse-skittering noises in the wall. I shiver and wait. Long into the bright night I listen, until I just can't stay awake, even waiting for the End of the World.

I do hear a voice. Two voices, in fact. I squeeze my eyes shut and hope I'm dreaming. But I'm not. I crawl out from under the covers. It's two guys. They loom over me, inches away. One of the guys is enormous and wearing a red plaid hat that matches my borrowed itchy jacket. The other guy is skinny. His Adam's apple sticks out of his throat and jumps up and down, like he can't quite swallow something huge.

"Thought I saw smoke here last night," says the fat one, poking me hard in the belly. "But Hod here didn't believe me."

"Okay, Tom." The skinny guy shrugs. "You win."

"Why don't you get out of bed?" suggests the fat one, grinning at me just a bit too hard. He reminds me of someone. I'm not sure who.

"We'll be back later," says the other. His eyes give me the creeps, the way they narrow when he talks.

"Sooner." The big guy laughs, the floor boards creaking as he walks.

They shuffle out the door, still talking.

"What's he doing up here?"

"Who the hell knows, but we'll get it out of him."

"Ayuh." The other guy cackles.

Crazies. It has to be.

I've lost my sister and Lenora, and now I'm about to lose me. I have to get out of here! I'll take the canoe and head across the bay. Stuffing some cans and the can-opener into an old backpack I find on a hook, I creep out on the deck. It's totally foggy. It must be way late in the morning, judging from the gummed up feeling in my brain. This is how I always feel when I sleep more than ten hours.

There's nothing scary in the sky. I can't even *see* the sky, or anything else. The world is just outlines. And then it comes to me. Duh. The northern lights—that's what I saw in the night—it has to be! I've seen them before, long ago with Mom and Dad and Shriek. It was different that time, more silvery and a lot less lonely. Mom said it was the solar wind blowing or something. The aurora borealis, not the Judgment Day. A cosmic joke! Despite my massive problems, I laugh. I'm a total moron.

I follow the worn stones down to where the water used to be. It smells like seaweed, but there's nothing there. I can't escape by canoe. No water!

The fog reveals only rocks. Nature's laughing at me. The tide is dead low. I forgot about the tides. Right now, there are only rocks and mud and seaweed as far out as the middle of the bay.

Little squirts of water shoot out of the muck by my feet. There are clams down there. I dug clams once with Mom, and then we cooked them up in a big pot on a bonfire at the beach. I sink down on a rock, wondering where to go next, but there isn't time to even complete the thought. There are footsteps crunching down the path. . . . I don't turn around to look. There's nowhere to go anyway, and nothing I can do.

"Good morning," says the big guy, lowering his big self onto the rock next to mine.

"Again," says the other guy. "Good morning again." He stands on the other side of me, arms folded, staring into the fog.

"Might as well say afternoon," adds the fat one.

"We've been arguing about you."

"Darn right we have."

"Tom here says he thinks he knows ya."

"Well, I do. I do. I did." Tom scratches his ear as if he has all the time in the world.

"Tell us your name, why dontcha?"

"Um," I mumble, "I'm not really anybody."

We sit there, and it's as if time stops. Gulls screech overhead, but I don't see them. A breeze flutters by. The sulfur stink of mudflats fills my nose. Nobody says a thing. Then the fog begins to lift. I spot the tiny island over by my family's side of the cove, the one I was never old enough to swim to. Then it's gone again. The north peak of the mountain appears for a moment, then disappears. The far shore appears, green and oddly near. Places come and go in the fog, like old memories.

The fat guy finally speaks. "See . . . it's like I told ya, Hod, he's a ghost." He laughs a long, deep laugh.

"A ghost like us." Hod guffaws, too, but not as if he thinks it's funny.

All at once, the fog lifts completely. Golden sunlight illuminates the mudflats, the distant water. Morning sun hits the mountain, turning it pink and gold. Dad always said we'd climb the Dagger's Edge together, the most dangerous trail going up to the summit. I try not to think about Dad and gulp back my thoughts, and concentrate on keeping my mouth shut. Ghosts? These guys are nuts. I'm not going to talk.

But they do.

"There used to be kids up here all summer long."

"Some kids in the winter, too."

"Remember the Toothaker boys, and that little Hannah?"

"No kids here now, ain't that right, Tom?"

"Ayuh."

"There's some that are buried in that mountain."
The fat one sighs, pointing across the bay. "Inside all
that evil."

I slide my eyes over to look at him. He looks right
back at me, and a tear slips down his ruddy cheek.

"People go in, and they don't come out."

"And only us knows the hidden door."

People? In the mountain? Hidden doors? What are
these guys talking about? I steal a sidelong glance at
the one named Tom.

"We weren't always dead, you know." He's looking
at me now.

"That's for damn sure."

"But, Hod, why aren't we gone if we're dead?"

"We're just still here, that's all."

"Keeping the secrets that need to be kept."

I decide to talk to them. They remind me of the lady
in the rocker—out of her mind but probably not dangerous. What do I have to lose?

"I used to live in that cabin over there." I point
across the cove to where the sun gleams off the roof.
"In the summer."

"Oh, yes." Tom nods. "They were a nice family."

"Lovely." The skinny one sighs.

"They used to buy our lobsters."

"Back before everything."

And then I remember them! The Rideout brothers!

That's who they must be. They had a lobster boat called the *MaryEllen* or the *MarySue* or something. They took me and Dad out with them once, and I threw up over the side, but it was still a good day.

"I'm Adrian," I say, so relieved to have figured all this out. "I'm Adrian *Havoc*."

"Yes," agrees Hod. "That's what you were called."

"Lovely family," says Tom.

"Too bad about the commandos taking over your house, eh?"

"Can't trust 'em," says Tom, shaking his big head.

"They don't trust us, neither," says Hod, standing up to fling a stone. "And they've got that lunatic in there with them. Told me blood was going to drip from the sky."

"Already has," Tom says, throwing a rock, too. It splashes and skips in the sea.

The tide's coming back in. I stand up and throw one, and it goes farther than theirs. But it doesn't skip.

Off their rockers or not, I decide I have to get Hod and Tom to help me. "My sister," I say, "my sister and my friend Lenora are somewhere. One's little, and the other's big. They disappeared. Have you seen them?"

PART THREE

Icy Hot

"The little redhead?" asks Hod. "Freckly kid?"

"And that knockout?" Tom grins. "The tall one with long hair?"

I nod. "Yes! Where are they?"

"Ah," says Tom, as Hod gestures across the bay to my old cabin. "They're in there, with the commandos."

"And the madman."

Fuck.

"I . . . I've got to see them," I insist, my mouth drying up with fear.

"Okay, then," says Hod, slowly. "We'll paddle over with you, but then it's up to you."

"We don't mix much, the commandos and us," admits Tom. "They've still got bullets."

I nod. Okay. Whatever. I'm only thinking one thing: They have Shriek and Lenora.

"We'll have to haul her out to the water, unless you want to sit here and wait some more." Hod's talking about the boat. The tide's coming in, but it's nowhere near the shore yet. It's going to be a muddy walk out.

We drag the canoe as the muck tries to eat my sneakers. We finally reach a thin skim of water, push the canoe out into it, and clamber in.

"Easy," warns Hod as I just about swamp us. The boat sits really low in the water. In fact, I'm surprised we float at all, considering Tom. He's enormous. But these guys can paddle. As we shoot across the bay, I wonder what happened to their lobster boat, the *Mary Whatever*. She probably ran out of gas. Like our van. Like just about every vehicle up here. For a split second I get that good old feeling—lemonade and fireflies. A picnic on the dock. Drops of water drying on my suntanned skin. . . . I trail my fingers in the water, then a jet rockets by over the bay, really low, and I remember I'm in a poisoned paradise, about to go confront commandos.

"Damnation," says Hod, nodding over his shoulder as the air shudders in the warplane's wake. "Big doin's at the mountain."

"Time's a coming," says Tom. "That's what they say."

"Stars are gonna fall."

We reach the little island. There's my cabin. Nobody's out on the deck or visible in any of the windows. My legs are shaking.

"Okay," I say. "I'm ready." It's now or never.

We ride the tide into the cove. The seaweed that streaks the rocks at the high water mark is shockingly close to the cabin itself. The sea must be rising. I scramble out of the canoe and give the Rideout brothers a quick salute. They paddle off, and there goes the canoe and any chance of a quick escape. I forgot about that detail.

I creep up the slippery rocks and onto the familiar deck, flinching at each creaky step. I peer in. The ladder going up to the sleeping loft is hung with clothes, including Shriek's pony pajamas! So, it's true. I lean against the glass and stare. My breath fogs up the window.

Ready.

Set.

I'm going in.

Whoever these commandos are, they haven't made too many changes. My mom's checkered sunhat hangs on the hook. The yellow butterfly I painted is still over the table. I run my hand along the countertop, willing myself back in time.

"I wish," I whisper, but a familiar voice interrupts my thoughts—

"Adrian?"

I turn to face a long-haired guy in sunglasses. My whole body goes icy hot with fear. It's the lunatic I saw pacing the deck.

It takes me two whole seconds to recognize my own father.

He's not on the moon. He's standing right in front of me, looking like a crazy man.

I'm so full of questions that I can't talk. There isn't much chance of that anyway, since right then Shriek leaps out of the sleeping loft at me, Lenora flies down the ladder, and they're crying all over me and squeezing me to death. My dad just stands there, looking old but like himself, too, now that I see him up close. He puts his hand on my shoulder.

"Oh, Adrian!" says Shriek, her head buried in my belly. "We were so worried about you!"

Lenora's holding me, and I'm holding her, and then I let her go and just look at her.

"It was awful," says Shriek. "I didn't know where you were. It's like you were already gone."

"We woke up, and you weren't there," says Lenora, her eyes drinking me in so deeply that I hardly stop to wonder what Shriek means by "already gone."

"Adrian," my dad says. He looks as stunned as I feel, even behind his sunglasses. He lets his fingers travel down my cheek and throat, and it's then that I realize that he's blind. He can't see me, at least not well.

"Dad," I say, choking back a sob. I press my face into his shirt. He strokes my hair. I look at him. I want to take the sunglasses off, to look into his eyes. But I'm afraid of what I'd see.

"Flash blindness," explains Dad. "I was there, at the blast. I can see, but things are . . . blurry." He smiles at me. "It seems you are taller now."

I'm almost as tall as he is. I'm glad about that. It would be too weird to see my dad for the first time in five years and have him be shorter. In my mind, he's so tall and strong. It's strange enough that he's scrawny and blind and without the military buzz cut he always wore.

"Your hair," I start to say.

"A disguise. Besides, it saves on barber bills." He laughs and puts his arm around me.

"We came here looking for you," says Lenora. "When you were gone, we just thought—"

"That you came home," insists Shriek. "Where else would you go?"

"It took me a while to figure out that this brave young lady was my own daughter," says Dad, as Shriek glances up at him. "Melody," he says, hugging her shyly. "I've thought about you so much."

"I have red hair," Shriek tells him. "Like the streaks in your beard." She doesn't tell him to call her Shriek. Maybe she remembers how he always called her Melody. They're both really formal with each other, and I can totally see why. Dad's like a stranger, even to me, and I was ten when he left. Shriek was only four and so lost in her daydreams that I remember my parents wondering if she'd ever talk.

"I hid the van in the bushes," confesses Lenora, snapping me out of my memories. "Your dad told me it would be best."

"This place is crawling with HomeState," Dad explains. "It only looks deserted. There's something big brewing up here."

I gulp, wondering if Hod and Tom are Them, and if I've blown it somehow by talking about my family. But it doesn't seem likely. They're the Rideout brothers from *before*.

"Let me start at the end," Dad says, striding back and forth across the cabin as the rest of us settle into the sagging couch. "I'm not here alone. Watson and Jones are with me, and a whole bunch of others—the Resistance—teams of us, scattered through the woods, even inside the mountain where HomeState is working on their dire plan. A fake Endtimes. That's what they're up to. They're going to make it seem like the Second Coming is here while they sell everybody salvation and false hope. There's a lot of profit to be made from fear and destruction. There's money in the God game. It's cynical and evil, and it's been going on too long. We're going to try to take them out.

"So, we're here on a mission. I'm with the Resistance. Adrian, Melody . . . even your mother doesn't know. It would be too dangerous for her, for all of you. It's better if HomeState thinks I died on the moon. But it's taking so much longer than we ever imagined. HomeState keeps postponing the End of the World. It would be funny if it weren't so grim. But there's a good chance that they're going to do it soon. Very soon."

Dad sits down on the couch to catch his breath. Then he gets up again, as if he can't talk if he's not moving. "Not being able to communicate with all of you has been the worst experience of my life. I am so sorry for it. But if HomeState even had a clue that my family knew anything, it would be terrible."

Mom, I keep thinking. She *must* suspect something. She can't just think Dad's dead.

But I don't say anything because Dad continues his manic pacing and his fast talking. And it turns out that he was on the moon for only three months, long enough to know that what the United Christian Alliance and its HomeState troops were doing in space, was setting up a military system capable of controlling all satellites and missile systems in the world. Then came a failure of enormous proportions, and he was there to see it.

It wasn't terrorists who took out Massachusetts.

"It was us," Dad says, shaking his head. "Well, *them*. Our own government. It certainly has been a convenient tool for getting people to follow their twisted version of reality."

"I knew it," says Lenora softly. She's holding my hand. We both sit there, barely believing what we're hearing. It's like I can read her thoughts, and they are my thoughts. So many millions dead, and our own government did it. Then lied.

"It was supposed to be just one bomb, one blast to bring unBelievers to their knees, to force those who questioned them to rejoin the fold. HomeState had it all planned out.

"We thought that we could stop them if we just intercepted the missile. We hoped to persuade them that what they were doing was crazy, unChristian. But we hadn't counted on their reaction. When we deflected that first missile out to sea, they sent others, targeting Boston and its surroundings. I was there, on the outskirts, when the bombs rained down." Dad sways back and forth in the middle of the room, caught in his awful memory. He wipes the sweat off his forehead and continues.

"The sky went white, so white. Brighter than the sun and louder than anything. The blasts kept coming. The heat was horrible, it knocked me off my feet like a wave. People were screaming. I've never heard such a thing. Buildings came crashing down around us. I couldn't see any of it, but I could hear and feel and smell."

We sit silently as we wait for Dad to keep talking. Shriek runs to him and throws her little arms around his waist. He pats her hair and takes a deep breath.

"I wouldn't be here if it weren't for Watson. He dragged me along, and we ran. My feet were horribly burned, my throat was scalded. Smoke and fire ate the city. We threw ourselves in the river and, after that, I don't remember much."

"But why, Dad?" asks Shriek. "Why did HomeState do that?"

Sometimes nine-year-olds ask the best questions of all.

"Fear," Dad says. "Fear is their friend, honey." He stops just long enough to look her in the eye. "Fear makes people follow, it makes them afraid to think for themselves."

"And that's just how the Regime wants us," adds Lenora as Dad nods his scruffy head. "Worrying about the Judgment Day and Jesus, instead of what our own government is up to. . . . We're up north in Maine because HomeState Command is not just on the moon, but also here. Here inside the mountain."

It's what Hod and Tom said, and I wonder if maybe they aren't so crazy after all.

"They've got people inside, working on their doomsday plan, involving everything from giant holographics to bombs." Dad rubs his eyes. "It's a rabbit warren in there, all tunnels and secret labs. We've got enough intelligence on them to know this much. But it's not enough. And there aren't many days left before the whole thing blows. We think they're scheduling this Endtimes Plan to coincide with what they call the coming Shift."

"Shift," I repeat. There it is again.

"In mere days now, the magnetic polar shift will

coincide with the maximum solar sunspots. That's why we've been seeing the northern lights almost every night. The earth's magnetic field will flip." Dad shakes his head. There's no time for the science lesson that would explain all that. "Let's just say that the polar shift is coming and the temporary chaos will feed their fires and fan their flames. It will knock out all ordinary communications systems. It's perfect timing."

"Jesus," I say.

"That's what they'd have you believe," Dad offers, wearily. "But the Resistance is hoping to take back the mountain, to invade under the cover of an air strike from the western front. You've heard that there's unrest there? Well, it's us. The Resistance. It's a long shot, but we have a chance. For one thing, we don't think that they're expecting us. The confrontation won't be pretty, but it has to happen, or we'll see fireworks like the world has never seen before—"

"And all in the name of God," Lenora whispers.

I can see Shriek working herself up into a little knot of worry. Her face is white and pinched. I can practically hear her words before she yells them.

"But Mom! Mom's in the mountain!"

Dad stops pacing and stares at her in shock. Shriek's thrashing around and screaming "Mom! Mom! Mom!" at the top of her lungs.

And right then the door bursts open.

Peace Force

A huge black man and a tiny woman so white she's just about see-through storm in.

"Shut her up!" says the woman, waving a gun. My dad gasps and scoops Shriek up into his arms.

"Jones, she's my daughter. Put down that gun."

"I don't give a damn who she is. Shut her up," she says, and by that time, Shriek's dead quiet.

Dad proceeds to introduce us to Jones and Watson, who aren't glad to meet us at all. I can see why the geezers called these guys commandos. They both have that military look, trim and tight. The look Dad used to have before he got all scrawny and let his hair grow down his back.

Jones gives us the evil eye, but after a while, Watson warms up to us and Shriek seems to like him okay.

Even though he saved my father's life, I don't know what to think.

Especially when he starts describing the plan in detail.

Three days, three days from *now*, they're going into the mountain to blast the crap out of HomeState. No questions, no prisoners. Just explosives.

"It's our only chance," says Jones grimly.

"Okay," says Lenora to me, when we finally steal a few minutes alone on the deck. "This is confusing. HomeState's in the mountain, about to broadcast some kind of giant Endtimes Rapture show in the sky, but there's this peace force alliance that's going to take them out?" She gestures across the waves to the gray-blue mountain. It glimmers in the rising heat of the day. "And the problem is, your mom's in the mountain."

I nod again. It's what Shriek says, and she's usually right. Lenora chews her lip and looks serious. I love her even more for not questioning my weirdo little sister. The way I'm starting to look at it, it's not so strange that Shriek sees stuff—it's strange that more of us don't. I stare at the water. The tide's dead high. Each little wave is a sun mirror sparkling with the illusion of a perfect summer day.

"He's out there somewhere," she says, a smile flickering across her lips. "Swimming free."

We stand there thinking of our penguin, looking out past the horizon, holding hands.

+ + +

Back in the cabin, Shriek's concentrating hard on something, despite the fact that just inches away, my dad and the commandos are arguing. The veins in Jones's pale neck bulge.

"There can be no change in timing. You know that, Havoc."

Jones takes me outside and sits me down on the woodpile to try to reason with me. "Your father is a brave man, Adrian," she says in a pinched voice. "But he's not right."

About what? I want to ask her.

"In the head," continues Jones, tapping her temple for emphasis. She keeps talking, but I don't seem to hear what she's saying. What does she mean, Dad isn't right? Why should I trust *her*? Eventually, she goes back inside to keep arguing.

I just sit there on the splintery logs, my mouth hanging open.

Mom's nobody to them—I realize that. She's just some scientist caught in the awful scheme. I run back inside. I've got to help Dad convince them that we need to get her out before the explosions.

"She's on our side," I blurt out. "She's only working for them because she's been forced." I'm starting to make connections all over the place. "The thing is, Mom's innocent. She's trying to stop them," I add.

"She's Resistance. Like you!" Suddenly, I know this for absolutely sure.

Jones looks at me with the world's squintiest eyes as Watson shakes his big head. "How do you know she's in there?" hisses Jones.

"We're not sure," says Dad, slowly. "But I think there's a good likelihood. Miriam is at the very top of the sequencing field. It would make sense that they'd be . . . using her."

"We *are* sure, Dad," I add, as Lenora squeezes my hand and Shriek doodles highly random designs on the back of an old paper bag.

"Well, we'll be seeing you tomorrow, Havoc," says Watson, finally, after nothing is resolved.

"The plan is the plan," says Jones, attempting an even voice. "You know that. It all hinges on Home-State's schedule."

"You sleep on it. We'll be back tomorrow." And Watson and Jones go off to wherever they go off to—to connect with other Resistance troops, or maybe to get away from Dad, who looks tense and like he's about to blow up.

We walk out on the deck.

"Is this place really crawling with HomeState?" I ask, remembering the aircraft.

Dad nods. "But mostly, they're over by the mountain, not down this end of the shore. When HomeState come around," he explains, "I babble about how the sky is falling and how slugs are pretty tasty if you fry them right, and that satisfies them that I'm just another wacko living out his last days in this radioactive paradise."

"You fooled me, you know," I say to him, tugging on his long hair. "I had no idea who you were. At least from a distance. And the Rideout brothers, too. Remember them? They think you're a crazy man." Please don't really be one, I'm thinking over and over again. But to me it seems like Jones is the crazy one. She doesn't give a shit about Mom.

"Hod and Tom." My dad nods his shaggy head. "Yes. I run into them from time to time and mumble whatever nonsense comes into my head, but I'm not so sure I'm fooling them."

"Those old guys? But they're nuts."

"Maybe. Maybe not."

"They said they know a hidden door." It comes to me, like inspiration. Maybe they can help us get in and save Mom before it's too late.

"Into the mountain," says Shriek, who has come out to join us. She's holding up her paper bag drawing. It's a complicated mess of circles and scratches. "I made us a map."

"Mom's in there," I say, as Shriek nods and Dad covers his face with his hands.

"I know," he says. "I believe you."

+ + +

And so it is decided that we have to find Hod and Tom, to have them show us the hidden door, to help us get in and rescue Mom.

Finding them proves unnecessary.

"They're already here," Shriek announces in her matter-of-fact voice. "In the canoe. Coming across the cove."

I don't see anything or anybody. Just the wide open water. But still, I hurry down onto the rocks. Sure enough, Tom and Hod are paddling toward us. At least I think it's them. At first, they're a faraway speck. Then they get closer and I can tell. Shriek's right. It's Hod and Tom, paddling—trailing fishing lines from the stern of their bright blue canoe. I jump up and down and wave at them. "Please!" I yell, "we have a question." Any HomeState guys hidden in the bushes are laughing their heads off at this point. But I don't care. This is urgent.

At first they raise their paddles at us, and I think they're going to paddle right by. I contemplate leaping into the water and swimming after them, but then they do a one-eighty and head into our little cove. They pull their canoe onto the rocks and follow me up onto the deck, taking their sweet old time.

"Doug Havoc," Dad says to the Rideout brothers, stretching out a hand in their direction. His hair whips around his face in the stiff breeze.

"I knew he wasn't crazy," mutters Hod to me. "I knew it all the time."

"Them commandos here with you?" Tom asks, pumping my dad's hand, looking around nervously.

"No," says my dad. "They're not here right now. And don't worry about them. Listen, we need to talk about the mountain."

"Showdown," says Hod, not without glee.

"Showdown," agrees Dad.

"About time we took the place back," says Tom, rubbing his meaty hands together. "Let me tell ya a little tale that'll pop your eyes wide open."

It turns out that Hod and Tom helped build the place. Not the mountain, of course, that's always been there. But the excavation, the labyrinth of rooms. It was years ago, before the Regime came to power.

"We were hired by these fancy people . . . told us they were a mining outfit," explains Tom.

"The money wasn't bad," admits Hod.

"They used us local guys," said Tom, "so if anybody blew themselves up, it wouldn't be them."

"Too dangerous for 'em," agrees Hod. "Them assholes didn't know their elbows from their dicks."

"Still don't," says Tom.

Hod and Tom lost their brother there.

"Amos. He was a good one."

That's when they installed a little something of their own . . . the secret door.

"We just thought it might come in handy someday," explains Hod.

"How about that?" whispers Dad, finally, patting my knee.

Without any hesitation, I tell Hod and Tom about Mom, and how she's in there, and how there is something big coming, and that she has to get out. As in the next day or so. Dad just nods, his arms folded across his chest. Maybe it's the wind that's making his eyes stream. He wipes his face and puts his hand on my shoulder. It feels warm and strong, like we're in this together. Screw Jones and her plan is what I say, only not out loud. We're going to save Mom!

"Be ready tomorrow morning," suggests Hod, as if he's merely arranging a little picnic. "Bring some food." He hops back into the canoe.

"On the late morning tide," Tom adds, hefting his gigantic body into the boat with the grace of a dancer. They push off from shore and unfurl the fishing line again.

"We're going far in," Hod says, or maybe "We're going fishin'." The wind takes his words so it's hard to tell.

"About time," hollers Tom, waving as they paddle off.

Sweet Torture

Trying to sleep is impossible. Dad and Shriek are having a snoring competition, and Lenora is curled up right next to me.

Then there's the fact that we're going into the mountain tomorrow. Shriek gets it, but I don't. She's been trying to explain. She gave me the torn piece of paper bag, covered in crayon and pencil lines. She keeps insisting that it's a map of the inside of the mountain.

"And that heart is where Mom is," she told me, in her quietest voice. "It's where you're going." I looked at the picture. The red crayon heart lies buried in a zigzag of lines. I put the map in the pocket of my jeans and tried to smile.

"Thanks, Shriek," I said, despite the fact that what she gave me is total scribble.

"You can do it, Adrian, I know you can."

"Yeah," I say, but that's not what I'm thinking at all. What about Dad? I know he can only see blurry outlines, but he's a soldier. He could do it. Or what about Hod or Tom? Why does Shriek keep talking about *me*?

When I can't take any more of lying in the sweaty sleeping bag thinking awful thoughts, I climb down the loft ladder and go out on the deck. The night is dark. The mountain is darker, except for the lights on the far side. A searchlight roams the blackness.

I'm standing there shivering, trying not to think, when the door slides open and Lenora comes out.

She doesn't say anything. This is fine. I don't want to talk. She wraps a blanket around both of us and puts her mouth right over mine.

No words.

Only kissing. Our tongues are talking, slipping in and out of each other's mouths, and I've never felt anything this good. It's an awesome conversation. Somehow I know all the words.

After a while, we stop kissing, and it is sweet torture just to sit together. Over our heads, the northern lights begin to play their colorful, silent song. Wild reds streak the night, and green sheets of light shimmer. The universe is way too big above us, but this time I am not afraid.

+ + +

"Anyone for pancakes?" asks Dad, early in the morning. He makes his way around the kitchen alcove as if he can see just fine. Practice, I guess. He's cooking pancakes on a woodstove. I can't do that despite my twenty-twenty vision. The batter hisses and leaps, and Dad knows just when to flip them. He always did. I used to love Dad's pancakes, and I still do, only he can't use any berries.

"There's too much cesium in the soil to eat the blueberries," he explains. "It will be a long time until what grows here isn't poison." I look at Lenora, who's looking at me, and we're both thinking of Grace Ellen's sweet little farm, with all its poison fruit. Still, the pancakes aren't bad, and there's some old maple syrup in the cupboard. "I've been saving it for a grand occasion." Dad smiles. "And this is it."

It's midday by the time the tide comes in, bringing us Hod and Tom. They're each paddling their own canoe. All of us are going. We have to leave before Jones gets back. That's what Watson says. He arrived in time for a pancake and proceeded to eat eight of them.

"Going anywhere near the mountain is risky," he tells us. "The last thing we want is for HomeState to think something's coming."

"We have two days," Dad reminds him.

"Then all hell will break loose," says Watson, licking the syrup off his plate, just like Shriek.

My dad nods grimly as Hod and Tom calmly tour our cabin. You wouldn't know that anything big was brewing, not with those two.

"Nice butterfly painting," says Tom, pointing at my childish artwork. It is very yellow, I do admit.

"Remember, Havoc," says Watson, stacking his dish on top of all the rest of them in the sink. "It can't be you going in. Your iris patterns are in their data system, probably your fingerprints, too. You'd set off their security system."

I look at my dad as he clenches his jaw.

"It's possible," he says. "We'll see."

"Don't be an idiot," Watson says. "Send in the boy."

I stare at the pile of dirty dishes in the sink. Why bother doing them? We don't even know if we'll be back. This is a depressing thought. I look at my dad. All I see is my own self, reflected in his sunglasses. Lenora takes my hand and squeezes it. I think of Shriek's map, like that's going to be a big help.

Watson stares right at me. Despite the clammy day, I shiver as he speaks. "Agent S—her name is Sylvia—may still be in the mountain, posing as medical personnel, most likely. She's about your height, dark hair, freckles, mole above her left eyebrow. If you can, find her. She'll be helpful. And tell her to get the hell out of the mountain with you. We don't need any martyrs."

I totally agree. Repeating the name Sylvia to myself,

Sylvia with freckles and a mole, I feel like I'm in some telejector show and they've hired the wrong actor. I'm no hero. I have the wrong clothes, the wrong hair, the wrong everything.

Watson squeezes the heck out of both my shoulders with his massive hands, but I can tell he's trying to be nice. "Watch out for that willful machine, son."

A willful machine. Great. That sounds pleasant. But I nod as we make our way down to the canoes with our daypacks. It's Tom and me and Lenora in one boat, and Dad and Shriek and Hod in the other. I concentrate on paddling, on not looking back at the cabin. I will myself not to think. The sun is high in the sky as we head across the bay toward the shadow of the mountain.

We climb out of our boats on the far side, and I'm already tired. The back of my neck stings with sunburn. I've never approached the mountain this way before. Dad and Mom always drove us when we did our day hikes. From this side, the mountain looks like the mountain, old and low. Nothing seems unusual, except a distant whining, rising and falling in a sharp, sad way.

"Remember," says Tom, as we haul the canoes deep into the buggy undergrowth, "if anybody spots us, we're out huntin'."

"Ayuh." Hod laughs. "Any season's hunting season

these days. That's one benefit to times being what they are." Both Tom and Hod have rifles, really old-fashioned guns, the kind that can bring down moose and deer.

I squeeze Shriek's hand and whisper, "Don't worry. They're not going to shoot animals." It occurs to me they're out of bullets anyhow.

She nods, but she keeps staring at the guns, her eyes huge and worried.

We trudge for hours, winding through the forest. Dad doesn't trip on a single root, despite his terrible vision.

"I'm glad Mr. Baby Guy isn't with us," Shriek whispers in a choked-up little voice. "This would be too hard for him. He would be slow."

"Mr. Baby Guy's as happy as a penguin in the sea can be," Lenora reassures Shriek, turning to smile at her. "He's chasing some sweet fresh fish."

And then, nobody talks.

From time to time, we stop to drink our water. I'm so thirsty, but I try not to take more than my share. The sweat runs off our faces, especially Tom's. He's bright red with the heat. We don't see anybody or hear much of anything, except the fierce bugs and us slapping them. Our arms are bloody with their corpses. There are strange sounds from the forest—munching sounds, rustling, and the sudden trills of unseen birds. I wish we could be on just an ordinary walk. Dad can identify the birds, even without having to see them. He knows their songs.

And there's that distant drone. It's louder the closer we get. It sounds like aircraft or caged bees and somehow like muttering, but I can't make out any words.

"They say there's something very strange in there," says Tom, when we finally stop to rest. We're under a huge boulder, covered in moss. The noise is coming straight through the rock itself. I get it now, and my heart skips a beat. Whatever it is, is *in* the mountain. I press my ear against the cool, old stone and listen. "They call it Gabriel," whispers Tom.

"The willful machine," says my dad, fingering his beard.

Hod and Tom both nod like people who have seen too much—slowly, without any emotion. But have they seen this? Have they been inside the mountain since it has been occupied by the enemy? What do they really know? I look at my sister and Lenora. We should have left them at the cabin. Well, at least Shriek. She's just a baby. But then again, Shriek is Shriek. In some ways, she probably knows more than any of us about what's in store. Her head is tilted as if she alone can hear the words in the grumbling drone.

"What is it saying?" I ask her softly, but she just

shakes her head and looks at me with eyes as haunted as old Veronica's in that dark kitchen at the End of the World.

Gabriel, I repeat to myself. It's the name I heard on Mom's strange telejector message. The message that made no sense. Isn't Gabriel the archangel who will blow his sacred trumpet on the Last Day? Mitzi made me watch a program on him once. It told about how Gabriel is the angel who chooses the souls who get to be born on earth. He tells them all worldly knowledge, then silences them—the cleft under everybody's nose is supposedly the mark of his heavenly finger. I told Mitzi that the cleft is actually a snot channel, and that didn't go over too well. The whole thing is nuts. HomeState is crazier than the crazies. Fake angels projected into the sky? Bombs for peace? Can people really be that dumb?

We emerge from the forest into a clearing. Long ridges of granite loom ahead. We stand there—six people, one mountain, and the hum. It's become more noticeable, but we don't talk about it.

"Here's where we split into two groups," says Hod. He is our captain, merely by taking charge. "Three of us will find the hidden door. Three of us will wait."

Lenora, Shriek, and Dad. Hod, Tom, and me. I want to ask why we're divided in this way, but I don't, and neither does anybody else. Not even Dad. I remember what Jones said about him, and it gives me a sick feeling. Shouldn't Dad be saying something? And what if Hod and Tom really are crazy? What if this is one stupid mistake? What if Mom isn't in the mountain at all? The questions descend on me, more persistent than the mosquitoes, and unslappable.

We split up the supplies in silence.

"Shelter in the hemlock grove," Hod orders my dad and the girls. "We'll send you a message before night-fall."

"It's nice in there." Tom sighs. "You'll see birds, I would venture. Maybe a rabbit or two."

"They make good eating," says Hod. "Right good with cream sauce, if we only had any cream."

"Follow the map," Shriek whispers to me. I pat my pocket. It's in there, for what it's worth.

"Adrian," my dad finally says, holding me in a strong embrace. I remember the smell of his sweat. Suddenly, I feel like I'm about ten years old. "I wish it could be me going in—"

"I know," I say, attempting a brave smile that he cannot see. "But you'd set off all those alarms. You've been one of them."

He shakes his head, looking way too sad and old. Then he hugs me even harder. "Trust your instincts," he says. "I'm with you every step of the way."

I nod, my mouth too dry to speak.

"We'll be waiting for you," Dad adds softly.

The girls and I hug, then I untangle myself and follow Hod and Tom. I keep my eyes on the rocky ground. They blur with tears. I blink and swallow hard, and try not to trip.

We're climbing. We're on a path that's not really a path. A deer path, Tom calls it. Branches slash my face with every step. Even though he's a moose of a man, Tom walks through the woods silently. As I walk, I'm thinking about Mom, only Mom. If she's there inside that hum, I will find her.

I follow Hod and Tom up, up, up, over rocks and moss to the sprawling base of the mountain. The whining drone is so loud it's getting hard to think. I hope to hell and heaven that I'm ready for whatever comes next.

100 Percent Chance

What's next is a rock wall. Granite covered in lichen and woody vines. It looks natural enough, but I guess it's not.

"Ayuh," says Tom. "Just like I remember it."

"Yup," agrees Hod, fingering a large, rusted lever. "Looks like this ain't exactly their front door, neither."

"Undiscovered." Tom nods.

"Nobody knew except us," Hod says with pride in his voice. "Okay, then—moment of truth." He grasps the lever with his bony hand and tries to turn it. Nothing. He yanks on it. Nothing. He wrenches it with all his might.

"Let me at it," says Tom, hefting him out of the way. He leans his whole body against the bar. Like a knife through butter, it starts to turn, slowly at first, then so fast that Tom crashes down, butt-first, onto the ledge. A small door groans open.

The humming noise pours out and fills me. It's not so much that it's louder, it's just that it's like we're inside the noise now, or maybe it's inside us. I take a long breath and stick my head into the opening, farther into the sound. The door is small, there's no way that Tom can go through, maybe not even Hod with all the bony angles of him.

But I can weasel in.

"Just a second," I say, taking the flashlight Hod's offering me, accepting the leg up from Tom. "Back soon."

I slither through a rock tunnel so narrow I keep bumping my head. Something tickles the back of my neck, a spider maybe. The air is warmer now. It feels like the tunnel has opened into a room. It's dark; I can't see. I listen for a moment to make sure nobody is there, then I pull out my flashlight and shine it.

What I see makes me gasp—rows and rows of limp people, hanging from the ceiling, reminding me of the body on the rope swing way back south. I'm sweating icicles, and I hardly dare breathe. I turn off the flashlight and wonder what to do. After a while, I realize that the good thing about dead people is that they can't hurt me. I decide to take a second look.

They aren't corpses, they're just jumpsuits, yellow

HomeState uniforms, hanging from their spandex necks. Lined up below them in neat rows are the black boots. I try to breathe normally, and listen for a minute. There's nothing to hear except the droning hum. I sweep the light around the corners of the room. It's a closet, really, and full of stuff. Crates, cylinders, uniforms. I wiggle completely out of the tunnel and drop onto the floor. I peel off my jeans, taking Shriek's crumpled map, with its squiggles and bright red heart, out of my pocket. I pick one of the jumpsuits and pull it on. I'm definitely tall enough to wear it. The material is stretchy, but unfortunately, no pockets. I'll have to stuff the map into my boot. I pick a pair from the long straight lines, and they are exactly my size. It's as if these thick-heeled shitkickers have been waiting here for me. Just wearing the boots makes me feel like maybe I can succeed. Now, I'll at least look like them. I scout around for some headgear. A HomeState cap would be nice. I shine the flashlight into every corner. I'm guessing that there's no genetic identification system in this area, or they'd be on to me already. With HomeState you never know. It seems like they're either state of the art, or dumb-ass stupid, and I'm voting for dumb-ass stupid.

On a tall shelf, I see a box of Munchitos, Daniel's favorite snack food of all time. I eat one. It tastes like salty cardboard, but I don't care. And right there next to the crackers there's a face mask, the kind with a ventilator. I pull it on and worm back through the tunnel, pushing the Munchitos box ahead of me.

As I crawl out, Hod and Tom stiffen and back away.

"It's me, Adrian," I say, pulling off the stretchy cap with its annoying mouthpiece. I offer them some crackers, all casual and heroic.

"Ya got me," says Tom, wiping his forehead, grabbing a fistful of Munchitos, then another. He crunches on them, looking at me with what I realize is respect.

We stand there for a moment, until I know that if I wait any longer, I'll be too damn scared to go back in.

"We'll be waiting for ya," says Hod gently.

I reach into my boot and retrieve Shriek's map. On one side of the mountain, she's drawn a big fat arrow. START HERE, it says in her childish handwriting. Okay. I will, I think, then I crawl back into the tunnel, giving myself over 100 percent to chance.

Holy War

I inch back into the supply closet and dangle my way to the floor. Steadying myself against a shelf, I catch my breath. My flashlight beam falls on a bottle of cleaning fluid and a mop. They could be useful . . . props. I'll be the janitor, somebody who might blend into the scenery. Time goes by so slowly that I'm stuck in the same minute for hours. Finally, my cautious flashlight beam finds the door. It opens onto a long, white hallway. I return the flashlight to what I hope is the same shelf in the janitor's supply room and try to memorize where I am. CUSTODIAL B., that's what it says on the door. From Shriek's map I know that the way in is not the way out, but you have to be smart.

Standing in the hallway, I hear footsteps, so I make myself walk. All of the doors in the hallway have metal plates, each with a number. Three HomeState guards round the corner, two men and a woman, fellow yellow jumpsuits. I've got my mask pulled down, though. They aren't wearing masks at all.

"That you, Jason?" calls the tallest one, laughing. "Going incognito?"

My small fake laugh wheezes through the mouthpiece, as I wiggle my mop at them to indicate hello. I don't dare peel off the mask. What will happen when somebody sees my face?

They stop by one of the doors. The woman touches the metal plate, and the door slides open. It's one of those fingerprint security setups. The three of them step into an elevator, the door slides shut, and they're gone. Sweat pours down my back as I rip off the mask and breathe for a moment. Then I pull my disguise back up.

I'm in, I tell myself. I'm Jason, maybe. He must be a guy who carries a mop. And this Jason is going to do some serious housecleaning. I want to pull out the map—it seems to me that the long loops and scribbles might make sense to me now that I'm inside—but I don't feel like I can sit down and just pull off a boot. Someone might come around the corner. I try to remember Shriek's drawing, but all that comes back to me is the red heart. Mom.

She could be anywhere—above me, below me, anywhere!

I continue down the white hallway and open the door to a stairwell. It feels safer than standing out in the open corridor. And forget about attempting to take an elevator. My fingerprints would probably sound an alarm. From somewhere above me, I hear the clattering of footsteps. I race down, taking the steps three at a time, holding on to the mop like it's my new best friend. I just about slam into this guy in a white shirt. He looks mega-angry—his eyes are cold as sleet. My mouth inside the mask keeps opening and closing as the ventilator makes a disgusting sucking sound.

"Take off the headgear, soldier," says the man. "Where do you think you are, in the Deadlands?" His voice reminds me of the football coach's voice at school and why I never wanted to join the team. Slowly, I put down my mop and the bleach, and peel off the cap. I try to look him in the eye. He just stares at me, and I wonder if it's because my eyes are two different colors and if he knows I'm a spy. "Don't you think you're running a bit late?"

I gulp back my fear. "Yes, sir!" I say. "Sorry, sir!" *Sir* is one of those useful words to hand to people in power. They feel they're owed it.

"Proceed directly to the level-one chapel." The white-shirt guy frowns. "On the double!"

"Yes, sir," I bark back. Guessing that level one is

— 163 —

below me, I grab the cleaning supplies and sprint down the stairs, the man following behind. He's walking. He doesn't need to hurry. I exit into a hallway marked "one" and notice that the hum is louder here. Farther down, deeper in. The hallway is just like the one upstairs, white and full of doors. There's a bit of mud on the stone floor. Is that what the guy is mad about? Is Jason late for mopping up the mess?

The man comes up behind me. "Go on," says his steel-cut voice.

I have no clue where to go, but just then, a yellow jumpsuit runs down the corridor and into a room. He looks late, too. I take a cue and scurry that way, the man in white following me like we're in a nightmare together and he's my worst fear.

When we get to the door, I step aside, pretending to be polite, but it's really that I don't dare touch the number plate with my unofficial fingerprints. I lower my eyes in case there is iris-scanning.

I follow the white-shirt man into a room crowded with fellow jumpsuits, and it starts.

Music. Really bad music. It's the Raptures or something. The music fills the room, drowning out the hum, but it's almost worse. This loud, it's like a weapon. The sickly sweet hymns pump into every cell of my body, and I wince. I find myself kneeling on the floor, just another soldier. We're all lined up and facing the far wall. It's a giant telejector. A familiar face grins out at us, then floods into the room. The president, holographically present and twice as tall. We bow our heads as he gives the familiar benediction of the flag— *May these colors fly over the entire free world.* Then the president is gone, and in his place is the preacher of the house. He welcomes us all and thanks us.

"To you who are about to embark on Operation Shift, for the Glory of Jesus and the Everlasting United Christian States, I say this prayer. Almighty Lord (he bows his head), *bless these young soldiers who have gathered together in your name. They guard the bastion of truth that lies in the mountain. They will herald the new age, they will bring your Word, Dear Lord, to the legions of unBelievers. And those that do not fall to their knees alongside us will be destroyed. In your name, and for all Eternity. Blessed be those who gather in the name of this Holy War."*

He goes on, but my mind is stuck on "Holy War." It makes no sense—it's the oxymoron from hell. As I sit there, trying to block the words from reaching my brain, I hear whispering behind me. It's the voice of the man in white.

"Gabriel is ready. He can perform the final sequencing even if she won't."

"She'll come around. What choice does she have?"

She. Must be Mom.

Blind Sight

I strain to hear more, but the music blares. The preacher's face morphs into the face of Jesus, at least the one that's commonly shown on the telejector. I always wondered if they got an actor to play him or if it's just a made-up face. His brown beard looks like girl hair, and there's blood dripping from his crown of thorns. Then he speaks, in a voice oddly similar to the president's, but I don't know what he says because the white-coat people behind me are whispering again, saying *tomorrow, tomorrow,* and that scares the heck out of me—I thought we had two more days. Jesus fades away into sort of a glorious indoor sunset, and all the jumpsuits shout with joy and go wild and weep. I wave my hands around, too, just to fit in, but what kind of wacko God would want this behavior? How is it faith if we're being told to think it?

More crappy music and we all rise to our feet to sing "God Bless Our Country" as the face of the president reappears, shouting about salvation. Why just our country? That's what I always wonder. The real God has to be too big for just one country, or even for just one religion, but this crowd is only rooting for the home team.

I snap out of my thinking and try to focus. I'm here to find Mom and get us both out before the Resistance arrives. I'm trying to swallow the lump in my throat, when I feel a hand on my shoulder.

"These sermons always get to me, too, brother."

I fake a sincere smile and take a chance. "Where is the woman scientist?"

The yellow-jumpsuit guy stares at me. He's used to following orders, I guess, not fielding questions. But he answers. "Um, the fat one, or the one with the silver buzz cut?"

I stall. Mom's never been fat, and her hair is dark and long. "Uh, silvery," I say. Stress can make your hair turn gray, I've heard.

"Probably where they keep all the prisoners. Second floor." He shrugs. "Unless they've given her to Gabriel."

I nod at him and notice that he's looking at me funny, maybe because he's never seen me before today and he wants to know why I'm asking.

"Right!" I roll my eyes, as if I can't believe how stupid I am. Then I retrieve my mop and walk out of that

— 167 —

cavernous room back into the hallway, then the stair-well. Second floor, here I come. I act like I know just what I'm doing, to fool the HomeState guys and to fool myself, and to avoid thinking about the Gabriel thing.

The problem is, I have no clue which door is the one to the lab. They're all identical, except for their num-bers. None of them say "Prisoners in Here" or "Possi-bly Useful Enemies of the Regime" or "Mom."

I decide I'll walk with my eyes closed. It's an old trick of Shriek's. She claims there are times when she can actually see better that way. She calls it her blind sight.

"How many fingers," I'd ask her as she squeezed her eyelids shut.

"No, dumb-dumb," she'd say. "That's not the kind of thing I mean. I see things you can't see with your eyes open."

It's worth a shot.

I close my eyes and walk. Slowly. Step by step down the long hallway, concentrating on invisible informa-tion. I don't notice the footsteps until someone's breath is right in my face. I open my eyes to see a guy about my height in the same standard-issue yellow, with a friendly look. It's disarming to see a face like that in a place like this. I blush and look down at the floor. Don't let him start talking to me, I think, or I might talk, too.

"You okay?" he asks. I wonder if maybe he's Jason, but he doesn't say anything about the mop. He just laughs and walks on. I shut my eyes again. I pretend I'm Dad. Concentrating like this, I get really aware of the hum. It's like the audio equivalent of a toothache, and I don't like it. I walk slowly until I stumble over my own feet. I take this as a sign. "Okay Shriek-O," I say to myself, "here I go." The door I'm standing by is locked, of course. I don't dare touch the number plate, and I'm standing there wondering what I should do next when an angry woman in a crisp white shirt rushes out that very door, almost knocking us both over.

"Soldier," she yells, as my stomach ties itself in knots. "What *do* you think you are doing?"

I cramp up in nervousness and stall. "I . . . just feel a bit faint. Um, sorry." This must be one special door. I've probably found the right room, only now I'm caught.

"Well," she sneers, "then it's the infirmary for you." Her face remains frozen in one expression, perhaps the only one she has.

"Okay," I mumble. "Thank you." I'm sure I'm a convincing shade of green. She leads me into the elevator, and we go up, I think. We enter a white room. Its biting hospital smell makes me cringe. I'm not sure about this. Then it occurs to me that I might meet Agent S this way. Sylvia with the mole. Watson said she was in health care.

"Ah, there you are, Doctor," the angry lady says to a man in puke-green scrubs. "This young man needs attention." The way she says that last word doesn't exactly make me feel better.

She gives me a final smirk, then marches out of the room, her pointy heels clicky-clacking on the stone floor. I face the doctor. His eyes are bloodshot and creepy. Instantly I want to be anywhere but here.

"What seems to be the problem?" he asks.

"Oh, nothing much." I look around the room. It's basically a white cave outfitted with stainless-steel cabinets and long rows of sharp-looking objects—needles and scalpels and knives. "I was a bit dizzy. I'm fine now. I'm good to go."

"Not so fast," says the doctor. "I must check your vitals."

Okay, I think. That's blood pressure, right? Still, I feel myself shuddering.

"Relax," says the doctor, smiling a little too hard. "I'll check you out, then we can say a healing prayer together. I will not release you until you can function at the high level we require of all our HomeState soldiers. Up on the table, private, and off with your uniform. Socks only." He frowns at me, pointing at an examination table.

Socks only? What the crap? I hop up on the table, despite my strong urge to run. The doctor pulls the curtain. It's covered in daisies and ducks.

"I'll be right back."

I start to peel off the jumpsuit, then realize that I have my old blue T-shirt on underneath, a huge tip-off that I'm not who I'm pretending to be. HomeState must have standard-issue underwear. I'm still sitting there when the infirmary door bursts open and a whole squad of yellow jumpsuits run in, with the white-shirt guy I met in the stairwell and the evil woman hurrying alongside. They're wheeling in a cart. Someone small is on it, strapped to the gurney and still as stone.

"We're losing her!" yells the woman. "We can't lose her. She's vital to the plan, and she hasn't released the final sequence!"

The patient's hair is shorn close to the skull and silver gray. It's definitely a woman, not a kid. Her skinny shoulders heave up and down. It looks like she can barely breathe. I cover my mouth to avoid crying out—

Mom!

Spiritual Matter

"Nurse!" yells the doctor, falling into a chair, "get in here!"

Immediately, a large woman crosses the floor, her brown eyes taking it all in. I peek out from behind the ducks and daisies.

"Get an IV going," blabs the doctor. "Stabilize her. Oxygen! Do something!"

"Step back," the nurse says in a calm voice that carries. "The patient needs air, and I need space." The white shirts obey, and the yellow squad is dismissed. They file out the door like kindergartners ready to get on the bus. The doctor buzzes around, until the nurse glares at him and he goes somewhere out of my line of vision. It's just the white shirts, the nurse, and Mom.

"Let us pray," says the voice of the doctor, from somewhere farther away.

"Forget it," hisses the white-shirt woman. "This is serious!"

But I remember Grace Ellen's prayer: *From the grip of all that is evil, free us.*

The nurse leans her big self over my tiny mom, muttering something about having to reverse their treatment, and what *were* they thinking, for the love of God. How could they expect a patient to live if they kept trying to kill her?

"Get out of here," she tells her superiors. "The patient needs rest. You can come back every hour. In the meantime, you can watch her on the screen." And from behind my curtain I am so grateful to this bossy nurse. And amazed. I wonder who she thinks she is, to face down HomeState like this? Then I realize. She must be Sylvia.

The thing of it is, they leave.

I stare up at the ceiling, with its pulsing blue lights. We're probably on a monitor somewhere. There's no privacy in this mountain prison, but, judging from what just went on, there's plenty of reason to hope for human error.

I slip off my examination table and cross the room. I've got to. Mom is hooked up to all kinds of tubes and wires. I nod at the nurse, who sits in a chair watching me with clear brown eyes. Yes, there's a mole above her eyebrow, just the way Watson said. I take a chance.

"My name is Adrian. I'm her son. I've come to get her out of here." I mouth these words, barely moving my lips. The nurse doesn't say anything. Either she can't hear me or she isn't Sylvia. I walk over to Mom and put my hand on her forehead, just for a moment. It's slightly damp. The vein in her temple flutters with her heartbeat. *Mom*, I think as hard as I can, not daring to speak. There's surveillance everywhere, and what I'm doing doesn't go with their script. But I can't help it. I keep thinking my loud thoughts. *I'm here. We'll be okay.* I send her messages of love through my fingertips. I will her to open her eyes. But she doesn't. She doesn't even move. Except for the jagged up-and-down line of her heartbeat on the monitor, it's hard to tell she's alive. Before long, the nurse comes over and stands next to me. She looks into my eyes and takes me by the arm. As she leads me back to the examination table, I hear her whisper, "Resistance?"

"Yes," I whisper back. "Sylvia?"

She nods, and relief floods into me like a drug. Mom may be strapped to a hospital bed and unconscious, but she's here. So is Sylvia. We are now a team.

Hours go by. At least, I think they do. I doze and wake up in a panic—what if this is the day the

Resistance army will arrive? The plastic woman keeps coming back to try to shake Mom awake. It doesn't work. It's so hard not to leap up and strangle her, although Sylvia plays interference the best she can.

"We need her now!" insists the woman. "The countdown has begun!"

"We'll get her there, Sergeant," says the nurse. "Just stay out of the way for a while longer."

"Now!" insists the woman, but she leaves.

The nurse is stalling, I can tell. Mom's in no shape for anything. She's not even awake.

The routine repeats itself. I doze, I wake. Mom sleeps. The nurse fends off the white shirts, who are getting more and more insistent and shrill. Occasionally the doctor wobbles back in, but she dismisses him and he always leaves to do whatever it is he does in the next room.

Finally, Sylvia brings me a mug of coffee and something mushy in a bowl. Maybe it's morning. I tell her I have to go, and she escorts me to a blindingly white restroom.

"To be sure, God moves in mysterious ways," she says, smiling at me. She waits until I come out, then leads me back, mouthing, "We'll get her out. You'll see."

Then I am alone again behind my curtain. I see her rubbing Mom's forehead with a cloth. Mom seems to be breathing easier. She stirs a bit. She tries to sit up! I want to go to her, but the angry white-shirt lady returns.

"Today you are telling us, Miriam!" she says and slaps her on the thigh.

Mom curls up into herself and moans.

The nurse reappears with a tray for Mom. "Now, I think you can eat this," she says, ignoring the Home-State lady. "Much more tasty than what's in that IV."

"Well," huffs the white-shirt lady on her way out the door, "whatever form breakfast takes, I'll be bringing her down to Gabriel in one hour. He can interview her, up close and personal." I don't like the sound of that.

My mom's eyes flicker open.

"It's all right, dear," says the nurse, propping Mom up and spooning mush into her mouth.

Mom struggles to one elbow. "Gabriel—"she begins to say.

"There, there," says the nurse. "One bite for Sylvia, then you can tell me."

My mother opens her mouth, but instead of swallowing oatmeal, she whispers, "He's scanning our thoughts right now."

"Well," says the nurse, "then he will know that I'm coming with you."

And me, too, I think. I'm going, too.

Nurse Sylvia bustles around. The doctor hasn't reappeared for hours, thank God. Sylvia starts giving me little winks and nods, and at first I'm confused. But when she sticks Mom's breakfast bowl smack in front of what must be the main surveillance camera, I get what she is trying to tell me. I stuff myself under the rolling hospital bed that I've been sitting on for who knows how long. I barely fit. She piles linens on top of me until I'm just a bunch of dirty laundry. "Oh, my, so sorry!" she says in a loud and forgetful way, as she removes the bowl from in front of the monitor. Then with one swift move, she lifts Mom on board just in time for the return of those irritated *click-clack*ing heels.

The HomeState lady.

"Is the patient ready?"

"Of course," says the nurse, calmly.

"Good," snorts the lady as the cot rolls forward with a yank. Underneath all the sheets and blankets I can't see a thing. But I can feel everything. First, there's a long ride down the hallway, then the electronic sound of a door. The swift drop in the pit of my stomach tells me we're now in an elevator, going down.

Down.

Down.

Down until I wonder how there could possibly be anything deeper.

The doors open again. Above me, I feel my mom trying to sit up.

"There, there," I hear Sylvia say above the rising hum. "Save your strength, Miriam." The whining sound is intense. It's in every cell of my body. I want to clamp my hands over my ears, but I can't move, or the lady will know, and besides, it wouldn't do any good. The hum is already inside me.

"This is as far as I go," the lady says in that voice people use when they're pretending to be in charge but are really scared shitless. She hasn't met Gabriel—I just know it. She doesn't have the guts. "You will cooperate, Miriam. Of that I am sure." She laughs this terrible laugh. "Remember Stevenson and Chai? They never returned."

I don't like hearing anyone say *Miriam* in that awful tone of voice. It's too personal, too much like she's offering her up for sacrifice.

"Well, I'll accompany the patient," says Nurse Sylvia. "She's not yet able to walk."

The HomeState lady clears her throat. "Fine. Suit yourself. You will enter a chamber, pass through it, and wait. Gabriel will conduct the interview himself, in whatever shape he chooses. After you have given him the codes, you will return to my custody."

And it occurs to me that if this Gabriel can read minds, then my mother must be working horribly hard to keep some small corner of hers secret from him. Maybe this is why she's so exhausted. She's already fighting him, and it's not even physical. It's more of a spiritual matter, and maybe spirit does have matter, and spirit definitely matters. My brain starts to throb. *Gabriel,* I think, *Shut up and leave us alone!*

Then, with a jolt, we roll out of the elevator and into the heart of the hum.

Open Secret

We're in a room pulsing with warmth and light . . . red light, deep heat . . . it seeps straight through the pile on top of me into my bones. It's strangely relaxing, but the weirdest thing is that the sound is gone, or at least, it's changed.

Instead of the hum, there are words. They were always there, but now we can hear them. I crawl out from under the bed, and listen.

> *look up and you will see*
> *the return of the Lord*
> *seven times seven is forty-nine*
> *your mother's hair will grow*
> *all things change*

The words are bizarre. It's like I'm thinking them, but I'm not. Am I?

Mom looks up and smiles at me, like she was expecting me and it's normal that I'm here. We're meeting inside our own thoughts, not in the regular world. Inside an open secret. How can this be? I don't even care. She looks better, much less pale. The walls drip with crimson water. Nurse Sylvia is listening, too, a look of wonder on her face, to the words that emerge between the *plip plop* of water. . . .

> *stars fall into the sea*
> *marmalade on toast*
> *and so the trumpet will blow*
> *and they say wisteria blooms in heaven*
> *this one, and not the other*
> *the northern hemisphere will go first*
> *now and not later*
> *rain and more rain and destruction*
> *penguins cannot fly*
> *something something something something*
> *   something something something*
> *Amen*

It's like listening to a crazy person, or Daniel's poetry, which I usually tell him stinks (although it does make me think). I notice that Nurse Sylvia is staring at something way down the hall, and Mom is looking, too, so I look down the length of the cavernous room and see him.

An ordinary man in an ordinary chair, familiar

somehow. He's a bit wavery around the edges, like a holograph when your telejector isn't tuned quite right.

"Hello, Gabriel," says my mother in her old, true voice. I hear it everywhere in the room. I reach for her hand, like a two-year-old.

Mom keeps her eyes on the man, who at fifty feet away looks strangely like my fourth-grade teacher.

"I know who you are," he says, right to me. "You share half our scientist's genetic material, yes?"

"Yes," I say, and pull the jumpsuit down to reveal my ratty T-shirt. I just want to feel more like myself. "I'm Adrian," I tell him, although he already knows.

"Adrian," says my mother, "I'm not dreaming you—"

"You may hug," says Gabriel, like a king on a throne. "I find emotion so fascinating."

I stand up and hold her, my tiny mom with the skinny shoulders and the reassuring vanilla smell, and she turns blue. Blue as the cove on a sunny day. I'm blue too. In fact, the whole room is blue, and it feels cleansing, even though I miss the deep, warm comfort of red.

"Indigo," says Gabriel, "is electromagnetic. You will not mind if I enter your psychic processes."

I find myself nodding. It's not a question, anyway. My mom buries her head in my shoulder. I feel her strength returning as she stands there, holding me hard.

Only Sylvia answers, asking, "Well, sir, what exactly are our choices?"

"Dear Miriam," says Gabriel, uncrossing his legs and crossing them in the other direction. His rumpled shirt is convincing. I half expect him to start quizzing me on long division.

"Not division," says the man, "but numbers, yes, numbers. As you know, I am in need of the final sequence, the one that you, Miriam, and only you, carry deep within that magnificent brain of yours. Rather like a rare and precious stone. Sapphire, perhaps."

"Well," Sylvia says, "if she's got it in her head, can't you just fish it out, the way you seem to be doing with all our other thoughts?" I wish I'd said that myself, or maybe I did. The blue makes it hard to tell who is who and what is what.

"Good try," says Gabriel, "but Miriam is not so simple."

Mom shudders, and the waves of her emotion criss-cross the vast chamber, piercing me, and suddenly her pain and fear are mine. "Don't hurt her!" I yell from the floor where I seem to have crumpled.

"There is no need to be loud," says Gabriel. "As you know, I hear everything. As a matter of fact, I can hear it before you even say it."

I'm shaking now, trying to block my own thoughts, trying not to think any thoughts at all.

"Not possible," says the man, rather smugly.

Maybe if I fill my head with stuff, with memories, with numbers, decoy number systems, then I can run interference for Mom. Baseball stats—that's what I'll try. On my fantasy team, Havoc is batting .630, Wilson and Simmons are tied at .520, and Feldstein is down at .320. What if I made it more realistic? How about .420? I'd actually batted that for a season's average, the year our team won the Atro City pennant before the disaster when I was little and still doing organized sports. It was cool. We won it on my double in the ninth. There were probably hundreds of people watching and cheering. It was July. . . .

I keep thinking along, my head whirring. I try to keep going, but a soft laugh cuts through all the crap and stops me cold.

"Very amusing. But it is not baseball that interests me now."

Mom steps forward. I hear her suck in her breath. She's walking toward him without even hesitating. As a man, Gabriel's not all that scary looking: middle-aged, a bit fat in the belly, his hair kind of thinning and slicked over. It's just that he's not a man.

"I would offer you a seat," he says rather charmingly to my mom, "but you humans require such solidity in your atomic arrangements."

"I will stand," says my mom. "And I will ask you this. Can you know God?"

Gabriel shifts in his chair. "God." Long silence. "Is God in this mountain, too?" He pauses. "I am searching my databases." I wonder if a machine can be sarcastic. His outline goes a bit more blurry, then, for a split second, he disappears altogether. Then he's back. "Yes. God. God is the perfect all-knowing, all-powerful originator of life and ruler of the universe. God is the object of worship."

"Yes, I know," says Mom, tilting her head like a polite listener. "But can you know God? Do you have a soul, dear Gabriel?"

There's a really long silence. Nurse Sylvia puts her hand on my shoulder. She's trying to steady Mom, who has started to shake, by steadying me.

Gabriel finally speaks. "A soul is for the living." He sighs a fake sigh. "And I am neither dead nor alive. How can I have a soul?"

"Perhaps a spirit, then?" Mom asks him. Slowly. Deliberately. "A spirit that inhabits you?"

I can't believe we're all standing here, facing down the most powerful synthetic brain on the planet, and it's turning into sort of a conversation.

"But of course I do," says the machine. "I have the spirit of every living being inside this mountain. You know that. From rat to man. And thank you, Miriam.

I have the codes I need. I squirreled my way in before that charming detour about God."

Mom's chin juts out. She throws back her shoulders. "No," she says quietly. "There is more."

"You will release all information," he insists.

"Tell me," asks the nurse. "What exactly is to be done with this information?"

"Ask her," says Gabriel from his chair, pointing at Mom. "She's in our service. She has been writing the codes for the signals I will send." His voice has gone flat, like an actor reading lines before he knows the meaning of the play. "Together, we are programming the righteous End."

Mom sinks to her knees. "There will be a simulation," she whispers. "The Ultimate Shift. The Final Coming of the Lord. Only it won't be the Lord, it will be a holographic show of immense proportions, riding the tail of the solar wind, using almost seven thousand satellites around the globe." She sounds empty. "I've been trying to stop it, you must understand that." She covers her face with her blue hands. The hum is coming back into the room, worse than ever.

"Six thousand nine hundred and twenty-four," Gabriel informs us. "And then everyone will believe."

"Believe in what?" I shout, finally daring.

Quietly Loud

"Everyone will believe in this perfect ruler," Gabriel says slowly, "in this . . . God of yours." He skips a beat, and his hesitation heartens me. It's almost as if he's human and capable of being wrong. It feels like an opening to me, a chink in his armor, a weakness. So I decide to try.

"But would a perfect ruler—" I start to ask him, just as Sylvia says, "And just how is a skycast phony Rapture the best way unto God?"

But he doesn't answer because at that exact moment, Mom announces softly, "God is Infinity and a half."

I smile. It's such a Mom comment, the way she always compares everything to numbers. But it makes sense, too. An Almighty God would have to be *beyond* what we can possibly consider, beyond the beyond.

"Infinity and a half," says Gabriel, scratching his bald spot. "This is utter nonsense."

"Well," Nurse Sylvia chimes in, "consider the paradox of the daffodil, alive but buried under the winter snow. When the sun grows strong enough, it calls the daffodil's name, and spring springs eternally from the wasteland."

It's such a weird thing to say, but I know what she means. Even the Deadlands will once again live. Someday. And rock is a miracle. Sky is a miracle. Just being alive is insanely cool, if you really think about it. People don't need fancy telejector shows to feel the awe, the big mystery of it all, the quietly loud power of the universe.

God?

The prayer that I am speaking has no words and no sound, but it is still a prayer.

"Exactly," says Gabriel, surprising me. "Paradox, you call it. It compels me, the way I imagine an unscratchable itch compels a dog." He laughs. "There is a soldier in the mountain with a mutt named Jo. He thinks about her floppy ears and silky coat more than he contemplates God." Gabriel gets a good laugh out of this. "Even a machine can wish for relief," he continues. "My specialty is not the oxymoron. I am not programmed for conundrums. But I cannot help thinking about them, running unnecessary loops around the oddest concepts. Frivolous waste of energy, really. For example, I have heard it thought that 'the opposite of a correct statement is a false statement, but the opposite of a profound truth may well be another profound truth.'" The machine furrows his human brow and smiles. The thought seems to annoy him in a good way. "Tell me, can this be so?"

"Niels Bohr," answers Mom. "A Danish physicist who lived over a hundred years ago."

"But how, how can it be?" asks the machine.

"Gabriel," says the nurse gently, talking as if to a patient. "Can't you feel the sunshine? Can't you hear the small birds in their bushes, just before dusk? Do you know the sight of daffodils growing next to patches of old snow?"

Silence.

"What is a daffodil?" he asks, finally. "I do not yet know."

"What is in his memory," explains Mom, "is only what is programmed there. That, and what he picks up from those of us entombed within this rock." She manages a small laugh. "I guess nobody has remembered daffodils."

"Apparently not," agrees Gabriel.

Daffodils. I think they're yellow and come in the spring, but I'm not really sure. Sylvia will have to provide Gabriel with the floral details. But I'm curious about something, so I work up the guts to ask, "You mean you can only think the thoughts of people here in this mountain and what has been coded into you?"

Asking is the same as thinking, anyhow, with someone who can hear your thoughts. I look at the man in the chair, he who is not really there. The willful machine.

"You are a prisoner," I tell him. "Just like we are prisoners."

Gabriel stands up. The color seems to drain out of him. "How can I, who control everything, be a prisoner?" He does not sound happy with me. I start to wonder if arguing with all-powerful machines is a good idea. But he keeps talking. "Tell me more, strange boy. Your thoughts are so different. They don't follow the straight lines that the thoughts of others seem to take."

I'm not exactly sure if this is a compliment, but as if to prove his point, I find myself thinking of Shriek. I close my eyes. Gabriel can hear me anyway. I guess that's why he was babbling about penguins earlier. It must have been me thinking of Shriek, thinking of Mr. Baby Guy and how strange it is that we're all up north. Life is so random sometimes and then it turns out that the things that seemed so arbitrary add up after all. The little things are the big things. Like how great it was to find that canned pineapple and the way Daniel used to make me laugh when we hung out at his apartment just joking around. I turn to look at Mom. I love her so much. And she's here. Whatever happens, I found her. Fear drains out of my body, and I just feel peace. I'm alive. Life is weird, but it can be good. I look up at

Gabriel, who is staring at me with an extraordinary expression on his face.

The blue light intensifies until it fills me like some strange and lonely song.

"Take me with you," says Gabriel, quietly. "And we will go."

I snap out of my daydream. Take the machine with us? It's got to be a trick. How do we know what side he's on? He belongs to them. HomeState is listening in, for sure, and we're going to get nailed. They have their codes now, that's what he said. It's all over. How can we possibly stroll out of that big blue cave into open air?

"Ah," sighs the willful machine. "You underestimate their stupidity."

Sylvia walks within two feet of him. His outlines are shimmering madly, but the look on his face is one of great and enduring interest. She bends over him. "We would appreciate your assistance out of this mountain," she says. "And we, in turn, will show you the world."

"But the codes," says my mom. "Has the information gone out to the satellites?" She puts her arm around me and faces our interrogator.

"Gentle sister." Gabriel laughs. "You who go where your fathomless mind takes you. Stop thinking now. Find the place deep within yourself where you can be calm. Find the quiet that lies within. I have tasted it, and it is true. Yes, the skycast Rapture will occur, but I have made a few creative alterations of my own these last few minutes. What shall be shown will surprise even the president." He laughs again. "Especially him."

I'm not sure if I want a surprise.

"Fear not," says the machine, looking straight at me. "It is time for Shift." Then Gabriel disappears from the chair and there's nothing there. "Take me with you," says his voice. "Take my memory."

"What?" I cry. "How can I? Where are you?"

"Just do what your mother says," orders his voice. "If you do not take my memory, they will recreate me and still forget to program me with daffodils. . . ."

The blue of the room is shifting to green. The hum is now a siren, sharpening its edge in my ear. We're inside the machine, inside Gabriel, whoever and whatever he is. It's insane. The three of us hold each other, clenched faces frozen, as we will our bodies to stop jerking. But the force that's taken hold of us won't let go. It hurts like nothing I've ever felt. It's pain beyond pain, ripping the air from my lungs and blurring the edges of everything I see.

"The memory," screams Mom, straight into my brain, pointing with great effort at the far wall of lights, now flickering in random sequence. "Get Gabriel's memory. Inside the red, the red—" She collapses on the floor as Nurse Sylvia tries to hold her up.

I turn to face the far wall. Walking in that direction

seems impossible. The waves that flood my body push every cell in the opposite direction. The red, the red, I repeat to myself, staring at the distant light, until I am that distant light and only crawling to join myself back together. I am broken, but I tell myself I must reach the red. Days and nights go by, or no time at all, and I wonder if I am dying and this is some kind of hell. I cannot breathe, my lungs feel like they're full of molten lead, but still I crawl. Each inch is a victory. Mom and the nurse are somewhere behind me, but I can't turn my head to look at them.

At last, I reach the light. To my great relief, the wall is solid. I pull myself up it, one sweaty hand at a time, my hands catching on the craggy rock. The red, the red glow. There. His memory? How will I know it? The red burns and crackles and surrounds me in cool flame. I reach into it, and the noise stops. The lights fade—the cool, slim oval fits my palm exactly. My hand tingles. I breathe, and Gabriel's voice fills my head, saying,

"Now

walk

to

the

far

end

and do not stop for any reason."

His words are stepping-stones stretched out with too much space between them. I can barely make them meet. But still I walk.

We all walk. Walking isn't hard. We float in the same direction—Mom, Nurse Sylvia, and me. There is no more blazing red, no more cool blue. Just a door into a passageway that takes us to a door and then a passageway. Gray rock. We are inside a mountain trying to get out. The corridors continue. There are no choices. One foot in front of the other . . . no more pain. But I'm so tired. Mom stumbles with exhaustion. Nurse Sylvia and I hold my mother's hands. In my other hand, I hold Gabriel's memory. We do not speak.

No Exit

In the hallway where we find ourselves, it's chaos. Troops of yellowsuits jog past us in full uniform, their faces buglike behind their ventilation masks. Weapons dangle from squared shoulders. A high-pitched alarm fills our ears. Soldiers turn to look at us but nobody stops.

"Assume your positions," urges a mechanical voice over the intercom. "The Shift is upon us. The enemy is here. We are under attack. Prepare to meet the Lord. Repeat: Assume your positions."

Mom and Nurse Sylvia and I look at each other. Gabriel lies cold in my hand. The tingling has stopped. I pull up my jumpsuit to blend in again.

"By God, they're here," says the nurse. "I knew they were coming." She takes my mother's hand. "It's the Resistance, Miriam. That's who their enemy is. We have been waiting years for this day. They have come to take the mountain and stop the plan."

And I want to tell her about Dad, but there's no time. "We have to get out of here," I yell, remembering what Watson and Jones said about explosives. "This is going to get ugly." And something propels me to retrieve Shriek's map from my boot, where it's been giving me blisters. Following the yellowsuits out just seems like an invitation to be shot by our own people by mistake. I don't want an ironic death—or any death at all. "We have to find another way!"

I unfold the wrinkled map, and we huddle over it. The yellowsuits have disappeared now, have assumed their positions, whatever those are. I put my finger on the red heart. I don't think it stood for Mom after all. This must have been where Gabriel was—the red cavern, the place where we just were. A thick black line pops out of the map and draws a straight path. Yellow dots dash madly off in the opposite direction. "The yellowsuits," I exclaim. "That's what those dots are! We're supposed to go the other way!" We can't go out the way I came in. Too many soldiers would see us.

I fold up the map and we run down the hallway, deeper into the mountain.

"How . . . can we . . . be sure that we aren't . . . going farther in?" Nurse Sylvia asks, her breath coming in gasps. "We can't stay here . . . must escape this place!"

But I keep running, and Mom and Sylvia follow. The way out might just be the way in—a paradox, an oxymoron—a possibly huge mistake. But still I run, and they keep following.

We reach the stairwell. I glance at the map. An arrow shoots us up into something blue with stars. The sky. It must be the sky!

"Run up!" I holler.

"But, Adrian," my mother says, pulling my hand.

"No," I say, for I am now convinced. We have to make our own way. The corridor I came in through is swarming with HomeState. They'd capture us at once. "We must go up!"

The three of us ascend the stairs, the alarm ringing in our ears. The mechanical voice repeats its warning, "We are under attack. Prepare to meet the Lord." We keep climbing until the stairs end and we're on a platform somewhere high inside the mountain. My heart pounds as I look once more at my sister's map. Oh, Shriek, I think, this better be one of the times when you're right!

My mother takes the map. She looks at where we think we are, the tiny rectangle under the blue starry sky. We stare up at a plain cement ceiling. There is no trapdoor, no hook to pull, no button to push. We're trapped on the highest landing in the mountain, about to be blown to bits by the people who have come to save the world, and us, if I wasn't such an idiot. We are holding each other, out of breath and far from hope, when I see it.

A butterfly, still fluttering, its wings beating uselessly against the rock. It's yellow with a fringe of blue, and shocking dots of red.

"A swallowtail," says my mother. Right now it's the most beautiful thing I've seen in my life. It's something from the outside, from the world, and it's trying to go back. But there are several feet of mountain between it and the outside air. Nurse Sylvia leans toward it, tears streaming down her face. My mother looks down at the map. There is nothing but an arrow, leading us only to wall. It makes no sense. Still, I carefully put Gabriel's memory disk down on a ledge and lean into the rock as the swallowtail beats its colorful wings against the gray. I push until my face turns red, and sweat is running down my neck.

"Help me," I yell, and my mother and Nurse Sylvia lean into the rock and push too.

Slowly, slowly, the granite starts to slide—unless I am hallucinating because I want so badly to escape. But no, it is moving! The alarm continues to ring from far below, the electronic voice insists we will meet the Lord. We huff and heave, the slow scraping filling us with purpose, the swallowtail dancing about our heads, and we are a force to be reckoned with. . . . Finally, the rock is an arm's length away. We have moved it. We push some more, and all at once it gives and disappears. We hear it fall until the sound is lost to us. It must be steep out there. Where the rock was, there is only black sky and distant stars. The swallow-tail flies out the hole and is gone into the night.

Fake Reality

The world is dark. Wind lashes my face. Below me, there is only rock, and far below that, the forest. It flashes with small fires. There is distant shouting and the sound of gunfire. The dull roar of aircraft whines from somewhere beyond the mountains. The night air smells like smoke. I claw my way out of the mountain and carefully lower myself to a ledge. I don't want to fall over the side and bounce my way into the ravine far below, like the passageway rock. Pressing my back hard against the icy stone, I peer into the darkness. We are at the top of the mountain. It will be tough to make our way down, even if we wait for dawn. There's room for my mom and Nurse Sylvia out here, but just barely. We can lower ourselves to the next ledge, I think. Beyond that, I can't see.

"It's okay," I call into the passage. "But go slowly."

After a minute, I see Mom's thin arms. She emerges headfirst, slowly, shivering already. Then Nurse Sylvia crawls through. She's a large woman. She groans as she crawls, and it takes her forever. Mom and I wait on the narrow bit of rock, holding each other and trying not to look down.

"I'm stuck now," Nurse Sylvia gasps, but Mom and I reach in and pull. She unsticks, and we teeter on the edge. Nurse Sylvia drops onto the ledge with a sharp intake of air, her white uniform ghostly in the night. "Dear God," she pants. "We're at the very summit. How in heaven's name shall we make our way down?"

"Slowly," I say, and prepare to lead the way.

We inch our way off the ledge, onto what seems like secure rock, twisting through the narrow gaps between boulders. First me, then my mom. Then both of us turn to help Sylvia. I wish I still had the flashlight, and then I realize that this is not the only thing I have abandoned inside the mountain. . . .

I gasp. "I left Gabriel's memory where the swallowtail was!"

We huddle together for warmth and inspiration, cold sweat dripping down my back. I am about to return to the landing, to make my way back up through the rock, when an explosion shakes the mountain. A huge rock crashes by, alarmingly close. We can feel it but not see it as it drops into the abyss below.

"No," commands my mother. "We must go on. Whatever Gabriel has communicated to the satellites is already done." We stand there trembling in the wind, remembering the surprise that he has promised. "His memory is already transmitted to the sky. It would make no sense to return."

"But," whispers Nurse Sylvia, "we promised we would show him the world."

The slim shadow that is my mother shakes her head. "He is nowhere and everywhere, a fake reality. A construct. All of us and none of us. And it is already too late. His operation was set to time out when the Shift started."

"Is it starting?" I ask, my nervous breath hanging like mist around my head. Time was impossible to tell inside the mountain, and, now that we are out, it could be any day.

"The level of sunspot activity and the extreme weakness of our magnetic field would point to yes," my mother answers, although I don't really get what she means. She sits down to catch her breath. "The only question is whether this will lead to a change in the rotation of the earth's crust, or to not much more than powerful northern lights."

We crouch in silence on our exposed slope, looking up into the universe. Stars shine their ancient light down upon us. There are no colors, no flashing flame.

Nothing is happening up above. It's down below that there is chaos. And it is there that we must go, to find Dad and Shriek and Lenora. To find Hod and Tom, and to get the hell out of here. Only first we have to actually make it down. My fingers are already throbbing and scratched from clutching jagged edges.

I bet this is the Dagger's Edge, if it's even any trail at all.

We huddle together on a flat spot, as Mom continues to explain.

"The regime is going to use this Shift to broadcast the Return of Jesus far and wide. They will send these images to all the world. Only those under impenetrable cover of cloud will escape this night of fear." She pauses. "The earth may well tremble as it likely did the last time Shift happened . . . millennia ago. If the earth wobbles on its axis and the crust shifts, HomeState will be happy. The president is safely in orbit. He won't return to earth until it's over."

"Earthquakes and tidal waves might come with this Shift," I say, "that will help HomeState scare people into believing, into following the Regime, into thinking they were right all along." But it all seems so stupid to me. Even if there are fires and destruction, won't people eventually realize that the world did not really end?

Unless, of course, it ends.

"However," my mother continues quietly, "there is

a distinct possibility that this Shift will be nothing more than a mild rearrangement, a time when we lose communications due to electromagnetic interference. Nothing more. HomeState knows of this possibility, too. The giant Endtimes show projected by all those satellites is programmed to happen before whatever celestial event happens next."

"When will we know?" Nurse Sylvia asks, rubbing her feet. I realize for the first time that she is making this treacherous descent in clogs.

"Soon." My mom sighs. "All too soon."

We continue down the mountain. Gravity is our friend and enemy, as we slide on the loose gravel, bracing ourselves against sudden falls. I bring my hands to my mouth and taste blood. Everything about me aches, but we have to keep going. If only I knew where. Shriek's map got us out, and now it is up to us.

We can't go south—that would mean climbing back over the crest of the mountain. Directly west, there is fighting. Now that we are inside the thick darkness of the trees, we can no longer see the flashes, but the sounds are so much closer. Shooting, yelling, explosions. It would be insane to walk straight into that. I have no idea what lies to the north. Woods and more woods, probably, all the way to the border.

To the east lie the sea and our old cabin. That's where we have to go. Dad and the others would try to make their way back there, too. I'm almost sure of it.

By now, there is half a moon by which to see the path, but I can't tell direction by the sky. We must head toward the dark distant water. I take a long look at it, then turn to face the forest. Branches grab at our faces and scratch our arms. We trip over rotting logs and crawl over moss, inventing the way down.

This is a path only because we are on it.

Endtime

We stop so often that it's as if we're going nowhere. Nurse Sylvia has abandoned her clogs somewhere up the mountain. Her feet are raw and bleeding. She tries to make a joke of it, but I can tell she is in pain.

My mother needs to rest a lot, too. She was never in very good shape anyway. She keeps looking up, as if the sky might tell her something. I just want to make it down and find everybody, preferably before the earth begins to shake or the sea comes in to claim us, or HomeState takes us prisoner. Urgency rises in my gut like spit.

"Please," I insist. "We have to keep going. We're nearly there." The path is no longer so steep, and the trees are taller, the way trees are at the base of a mountain. We are getting somewhere, after all.

We come out into a little clearing. At the far side, there is movement. I squint and see three deer grazing at the field's edge. One looks up at us, ears flickering. Then they all look up at us, and run off.

"So beautiful," says Nurse Sylvia, and I remember that there is beauty. Not just evil. We cross toward where the deer were, Nurse Sylvia exclaiming with relief over the wet grass. "This will soothe my poor toes," she says bravely as she limps across the meadow. My mother tilts her head toward the sky and puts her hand on my shoulder. I stop walking and look up.

"It's starting," she says.

A great whip of green blots out the stars, white lights shoot through the distance like celestial snakes.

"The aurora," says Nurse Sylvia with some relief, but it's the northern lights beyond what I have yet seen or imagined. It's like a telejector version, so three-dimensional that I half expect the color to rain down on us and the rising wind to blow us all off this little rock of a planet.

"Sun cycles have produced this," explains my mother. "We still don't know what Gabriel has in store for us with the Endtimes show."

We crane our necks in shocked admiration at what is happening above us. The giant curtain of green ripples with blazes of red. The white snakes crawl this way and that, then disappear, as waves of purple crash silently through the sky. I'm glad I'm not alone. But it's still just the lights, the aurora. And it makes me think. "Mom, how could HomeState think their plan was going to work? I mean, it's not night at the same time all over the world—"

"Over the part of the world that matters to them," she answers. "They do not see beyond their own borders."

We stand there for a long time, waiting for the fake end of the world.

"Dad," I begin to tell her, but just then the white horse appears above us, thousands of miles high. Its mighty hooves tread the night, his nostrils snort with fire. On his back sits an angry-looking Jesus. He is here to judge us, says the look on his face.

"Oh, no!" gasps my mother. "It's their plan. Gabriel didn't change it."

As the white horse and its rider thunder noiselessly by, Bible verses about repentance and death fly into my mind. And I don't even believe in Revelations! I wonder what is happening in the minds of those who do. Down in the valley, the sound of explosions and shouting is gone, replaced by only the howl of the wind. Both HomeState and the Resistance must have stopped to look up. It's impossible not to stare. What is happening above us is unbelievable. I drop to my knees in astonishment.

"Lord Almighty," says Nurse Sylvia. "What will be next?"

"The red horse," I guess, remembering the message on my mother's screen. "The one that brings us death."

And red begins to gather, high above us in the pulsing heavens. But there is something wrong with the graphics, or maybe this *is* what Gabriel intended. The horse never forms. In its place is a laughing fat man, sitting on his feet. He looks both calm and happy, like he's finally understood a joke. He looks familiar somehow.

"The Buddha," exclaims Nurse Sylvia. She's old enough to have learned about other religions, the ones that are forbidden now. I stare up at the Buddha, wondering what he has to say. He takes up just about the entire sky, but the stars twinkle through him. Despite his size, he's not scary. He definitely isn't here to wield a sword, that much is clear.

"Good for Gabriel." Mom laughs. "He's accessing some of the alternate graphics I supplied to him. The projections will depict symbols of all the major religions. . . ." She explains that most adults will know what the images stand for. It wasn't that long ago that people had the freedom to worship in any way they chose in our country, or not to worship at all. "This will remind them," she says. "Of the freedoms that were, and the other places that are."

"If it doesn't scare them to death first," whispers Sylvia.

The giant sky Buddha evaporates, leaving a ghostly afterimage the way fireworks do, and in his place is a large, elephant-headed creature in a glowing crown, riding on the back of a rat and a beautiful woman with a whole bunch of arms, seated on a tiger. Golden blossoms swirl around her. It's awesome and hilarious at the same time.

"Ganesh," says my mother. "He is the Hindu god of wisdom, and Devi, the mother goddess."

There are voices nearby, and I have the vague impulse to strip off my HomeState jumpsuit so I don't look like one of Them, but at the moment I don't care about anything except what's in the sky.

The elephant guy and the astonishing lady are gone, replaced by an outstretched scroll covered in markings that look like an alphabet of crow's-feet. But I remember what it is.

"The Torah," I cry. Daniel's family kept one hidden. They showed it to me once. His dad was teaching him to read the ancient language.

"It's the same as your God," I remember his mother saying. "The Christian God and the Jewish God are the same, you know." I didn't know that, but it made sense to me. God is God is God, or how could God be God?

I put my head in my hands and for a long, deep moment think of the Feldsteins. Wherever Daniel is, I hope he's looking up. Maybe he's seeing this great Torah in the sky, right now, this very evening.

The enormous shimmering parchment scrolls by for a long while, its letters telling the old stories, then melts into a nothingness so profound it's frightening. When the scroll is gone, there aren't even stars. But then, the void updates itself into an enormous crescent moon and star, shining fiercely above us. I search the sky for the rim of the ordinary moon, but it has been eclipsed by this other moon.

"Islam," says my mother. She explains how it means surrender—"submission unto God"—and I wonder how that's really any different from what the telejector preachers tell us to believe. Then the crescent dissolves and a strange angel with enormous wings flies by, only to be replaced by what looks like Shriek spinning and twirling, just a hell of a lot bigger, extending her hand to a dapper penguin. Mr. Baby Guy, in his handsome tuxedo, hops about like he's ready for the ball to begin, and they have their cosmic dance and disappear. A daydream, bigger than life. Now the sky is crowded with flickering dancers and forgotten animals. Maybe somewhere, these animals still roam free. A giraffe, a hippo, and some kind of antelope. . . . Animals, just animals, chasing each other through the heavens. It's wild!

My neck is stiff from looking up. I swivel my head around, shaking myself loose. All around us, there is immense quiet. I realize that this is our chance. The fighting has stopped. It might continue again when this skyshow ends.

"Let's go," I say, yanking Mom and Sylvia toward an opening in the forest. We're edging toward morning, and it's getting easier to see the trail. "We must find Dad and the others."

Mom's eyes widen. "Douglas? He's here?" I can't tell if she's panicking or glad.

"Yes," I say. "Come on!"

We set off through the dark woods as fast as three exhausted people, including one with no shoes, can go. I realize how selfish I've been and offer Sylvia my Home-State boots. They're way too big and she protests, but I stuff them with moss and make her take them. She calls it a huge relief. My bare feet aren't tough enough for the jabbing rocks and roots, but I pretend that I'm fine. "Piece of cake," I say, gasping.

"Your father," pants Mom as she struggles to keep up, "is he really here?"

"He is, at least he was," I say. "I mean, yes." They *have* to be here. Through the treetops above, I see great ships in the sky, their sails unfurled to some cosmic wind, and then glimpses of daffodils. I remember how yellow they are. A little later on, there is a giant hurling a thunderbolt, and a long-haired woman on a horse.

"How did Gabriel get all these images?" I ask as we smash through the undergrowth.

"From all of us, I would imagine," says my mom.

"Are we thinking this?" asks Sylvia. "Or is it real?"

"It doesn't matter," says my mother, and collapses.

After Life

Nurse Sylvia sinks to her knees. "She's fainted," she declares, her head on my mother's chest, her fingers on the pulse in her wrist. "She's only fainted."

"Mom," I cry, straight into her ear, "wake up . . . please!"

But Mom doesn't, and we sit there on the damp pine needles, the last acts of the skyshow still flickering above us. I make out a floating pink pig and what looks like a giant teapot, but the images have gone all runny as light starts to gather in the east. From not too far off, I hear gunshots, freaking me out—the fighting might start again—but then there is long, empty silence.

"Don't worry," Sylvia says. "She'll be okay." Her voice is sad and tired, though.

We could use some rest. It's almost day. We haven't

found Dad and the girls. The fighting might be over or it might start again. My feet burn with cuts, and I'm so thirsty. My eyes can't stay open anymore. I lie down next to Mom.

I open my eyes to a high-pitched squeal. "Mom, Adrian, wake up!" It's Shriek! She's dancing around us. "I knew you'd be in this part of the woods!"

Dad is here, too, bending over us, scooping my mom into his arms—the dream I never dared dream.

"Oh, Miriam," he says. "It's really you." His hands follow the curve of her cheek and trail down her neck. And she recognizes him despite his straggly hair and bristly beard, and he knows her even though he can't really see her. They kiss for a long time, crying and whispering, and kissing some more. I look away, wanting to see Lenora, but she isn't here.

"We can't find her," Shriek says, shaking her head. "Not anywhere." She pulls on my arm and makes me stand up. I feel dizzy. "She went away in the night. Somewhere with Hod and Tom. I think she was trying to find *you*. But now we can't find her, or them." Shriek's eyes are anxious and I feel sick to my stomach. Lenora! She has to be okay. "But at least we found you!" She wraps her little arms around my chest and squeezes like crazy.

"Are you Sylvia?" my father asks the nurse, standing

up to shake her hand then reaching out to hug her. "Watson told us about you."

"Watson," Sylvia says, smiling broadly. "Glad to hear he's still around." Then we're all suddenly silent for a while, as it strikes us that he isn't. At least not here.

"We have to leave the mountain," says my dad. "It's quiet now, but you never know. This stunned silence will wear off, and too many of those idiots have guns."

"Where are we going?" asks Shriek.

"For now, back to the cabin to rest and eat," says Dad.

It's a long walk back to where we left the canoes. We take the most hidden paths, hardly paths at all, yet compared to our nighttime slide down the mountain, it's a walk in the park. We catch glimpses of yellow uniforms through the trees, but the enemy seems to be milling around, each man for himself. Some lie on the ground, dead or asleep. We don't see anybody and I wonder who the Resistance was, exactly, and where they have gone. After a while, we come upon a HomeState guy sitting on a rock. He looks up at us with fearful eyes. I look nervously at the weapon lying at his feet.

"Strange stuff in the sky," he whimpers.

We nod our agreement, but nobody speaks.

"Is this the Afterlife?" he asks us, as serious as anything.

"Yes," says Sylvia firmly. She reaches for his shiny

gun. He hands it over without a word. We leave him slumped on his rock, staring after us as if this is absolutely not how he imagined angels.

We stagger through the early light until we reach the inlet where we hid the canoes. They are still where we left them, their cheerful plastic colors shining through the undergrowth. Someone rises up from behind a tree and we all gasp. It's Lenora! She limps over to us. I hug her, carefully. She hugs me, too.

"Hod brought me back here," she explains. "I would never have found my way."

"What happened to your leg?"

"It's okay," she says, although there's a gash straight through her jeans and blood on her calf. "I think I fell. I can hardly remember. I was too busy looking up at the sky."

"Sylvia can help you," I tell her. "She's a nurse. We're going back to the cabin."

There's so much more to say that mostly we just look at each other. All I know is, wherever I'm going, she's going, too. I reach up and untangle a twig from her hair.

"Should we leave one for Hod and Tom?" my dad asks, gesturing toward the canoes and then at me. I like that he's asking me, but I don't have a clue. I shrug. I want to say yes, leave one. Hod and Tom have to be okay. But the six of us would sink one canoe, and everybody's in really crappy shape. It's miles to the cabin by land, but not too far by sea. We have to take them both.

"They'll be okay," I say. "They know their way. This is their home."

Dad nods. It's decided. But before we can go, we must wait for the tide. We hide in the bushes with the canoes, in case of wandering HomeState guys who still have weapons. The sunrise is shockingly deep. There is a fire burning to the east. The sun pulses as it rises. The incoming waves glow red.

"Please, God, let this just be morning," says Sylvia.

"What *is* this?" Dad asks. "It's already so hot." Beads of sweat run down his nose and into his beard.

"Shift," replies Mom. "This might just be true Shift. The timing is right. The earth's magnetic field has been dwindling for decades. We are overdue for a magnetic correction. With the solar wind as strong as it is, this could be a polar shift as well as a magnetic shift. It hasn't happened for at least 730,000 years, if it ever happened at all. There is controversy over that. But if it's happening now, we'll know all too well. . . ."

I stare into the violent sky as Mom keeps talking. She says all communications networks will fail, that satellites will be knocked out. There may be earthquakes and volcanoes, as the earth's crust crumples and slams up into itself. There will be new mountains and terrible rifts. Her voice is hardly more than a whisper.

"Will we die?" asks Shriek, her eyes reflecting the red light. "How can we die now? We're all together again." She sticks her thumb in her mouth, the way she hasn't done for years.

Mom envelops Shriek in a giant hug, kissing the top of her sweet red hair. I crawl into the jumble of them, and Dad, too. Lenora and Sylvia fold us into their arms, and we stay like that for a long time. Finally, Mom talks again, and her voice has more emotion. "The truth of the matter is, we just don't know."

"So," says Dad, like an echo, "we'll just take it one step at a time, okey dokey?"

"Yup." Shriek takes her thumb out of her mouth with a wet pop and announces, "It's going to be okey dokey."

I stare out at the water until my eyes ache with the glare. Closing my eyes doesn't help much. The insides of my eyelids burn with the rising sun.

Finally, the tide is high enough and we haul the canoes out and start dragging them toward the water. It looks like blood.

It's hard for Lenora to walk in the muck with her sore leg, so I steady the boat and make her get in. The mudflats are just slippery enough for me to push her along. The cold squishiness feels good on my suffering feet. By the time we're afloat, I'm slick with sweat, and it's hotter than I've ever felt it. A total scorcher, worse than an Atro City summer day.

"There will be drinks at the cabin, right?" Shriek asks, then she puts her head down on the seat in Mom and Dad's canoe, and is instantly asleep. Mom holds her, then she's drifting off herself. She's still so weak. Sylvia's in their boat, too, matching her strokes to Dad's, steering them toward the cove. Lenora and I do our best to paddle in a straight line, against the incoming tide. Lenora's strong, but she sucks at paddling and we keep turning around in circles. Heat shimmers up off the water. The horizon is a long streak of orange, and it's hard to tell where the sky takes over from the sea. The small breeze is nothing but wafting hot air. We keep splashing ourselves with the water, just to stay cool.

"If this is Shift, he'll just have to be a tropical penguin," says Lenora, over her shoulder at me. "A tropical northern penguin."

I search the waves for any sight of him. Will he survive? Will he be lonely? Does he even know *how* to catch a fish? Right now, I'm not sure which is worse—Dr. Septic and the needle, or life after Shift, but I have to believe we didn't bring him all this way just to die.

"Mr. Baby Guy," I say, as I dip my paddle into the strange sea. "Be fine. Swim free."

Begin Again

By the time we reach the cabin, the world is an oven, and the sun is only halfway into the sky. We haul the boats high up onto the rocks and crawl off to sleep, after sharing a few cans of water. Each lukewarm sip is the best thing I've ever tasted. Nobody talks. We're all way too fried.

I wake up on the kitchen floor. Someone has stuffed a rolled-up towel under my head. I look out the window. The sky is a scalding gray, tinged with blood-red clouds. I get up, stepping over Sylvia, who lies on her side snoring softly. Lenora's asleep on the couch. I'm guessing that everyone else made it up into the loft.

"Now I've seen everything," says a familiar voice from outside, "and then some. Pictures in the sky, penguins in the Gulf of Maine, a morning that lasts all afternoon. . . ." I go out on the deck. Hod and Tom are back!

My dad is sitting on the railing talking to them. They're passing a can of water around as if it is beer. They both look rumpled and saggy, but that's how they looked in the first place.

"Hey!" I say, smiling as Tom wraps me in a smelly bear hug. "You're okay!"

"Damn right," he says. "Despite their foolish plans."

"I'd laugh," says Hod, "even though it wasn't the least bit funny."

"Maybe a little funny," Tom says, releasing a world-class burp.

"If I met the president, I'd laugh in his face," says Hod. "His little show didn't turn out the way he planned."

"And now this," says Tom, spreading his arms out to indicate the world. It looks different somehow, and the same. For one thing, the tide is high. Really high. The waves lap at the rocks, so near the cabin, a raft of seaweed bobbing in the bay. The air smells like rotting stuff. A small flock of gulls swirl and squawk and settle on the little island, then lift again, screeching their own prophesies to the brutal breeze.

"Herring gulls," says Dad, who can tell just by listening.

The mountain looks far away and quiet. The sun seems to hang still in the sky, piercing a golden hole in the curtain of clouds.

"It hasn't moved for hours," says Hod, scratching his chin. "It's stuck, or maybe we're not moving."

"Now ain't that confusing?" says Tom.

"And unlikely," mutters Hod. "Must be one of them optical illusions."

Thinking of what Mom said about Shift, I hope he's right. What if the earth's crust has really moved? Could north be south and east be west? Is the magma supporting the earth under our feet having a high tide of its own? The world has gone bizarre, but my dad seems strangely calm. I flash back to what Jones said about him, but I don't think he's nuts. He just can't see much, so he has to wait and weigh all the evidence. And that might not be such a bad idea. I look out to sea. No tidal waves yet. The mountain hasn't crumbled. There's not much going on.

"So what are you gentlemen going to do next?" Dad asks the Rideout brothers.

"Well, probably 'bout the same as always," says Tom. "Hunt, fish, look for mushrooms."

I guess they're not panicking.

"So you're staying, then?" Dad asks, as if it were the end of an ordinary summer and we were getting ready to leave.

"Where else is there?" asks Hod. "If you don't want to live with fools?"

He's got a point there. Atro City and the Citylands must be a total mess. If everything electronic is out, there's got to be chaos. People will be going crazy without their telejectors and cells and everything. I hope we're not going back there, and not only because we'd have to cross the Deadlands to do it.

By evening, Lenora has had her leg bandaged up in dishtowels and duct tape by Sylvia. I've found some old jeans of Dad's to wear, instead of the yellow uniform. We've inhaled a buffet of canned stew and chowder and instant noodles.

"That's about it for the cupboard," Mom says, running her hands along the empty shelves. "Only thing left is a can of diced ham."

I guess we can take it with us, because it seems like we're going. Somewhere. Unless we're willing to eat radioactive animals and plants, like the Rideouts are, then we can't exactly stay here. I tell everyone about the cans over at the little cabin on the point. We'll get those, too.

We're sitting around the small table, starting to talk about what comes next, when there's a pounding at the door. Watson stumbles into the cabin, looking worse than any of us. His face is gray and he's all hunched over. Sylvia races to his side as he collapses on the couch. I open up the ham and offer it to him. He spoons it straight. Within seconds it's gone. He groans and shuts his eyes as we huddle around him. The sun makes its slow way across the large windows to sink behind the mountain like it always does. There's an evening breeze, and to everyone's relief, it's not so hot. The sea and sky are purple now, and darkening fast. Mom digs out a candle.

"Last one," she says. "We're out of everything."

"Except each other," says Shriek, reaching for us.

We gather in a small circle, the candlelight flickering on our faces. Mom and Dad sit close to each other, her leg hooked over his. They both look so old and different. Mom's close-cropped prisoner hair will grow out, I guess. She told me they shaved it inside the mountain, but she wouldn't say why. I'm sure it wasn't good. And Dad with his scraggly bird's nest. He takes off the sunglasses and rubs his eyes. They still look like mine—one brown and one blue.

I sit next to Lenora. Her thigh presses into mine. She and Shriek play a cat's-cradle game with some old string.

"I can make a penguin," says Shriek, looping the string in and out of Lenora's outstretched fingers. It's good to hear them laugh.

Watson wakes up, shakes himself to a sitting position, and starts to talk. "Oh, man. What a night."

"Indeed," Dad agrees. "This is my wife, Watson."

They take each other's hands and nod.

"I'm so glad you are safe," says Watson, his voice deep and solemn. "Things didn't go exactly as we planned." He shakes his head in bewilderment. "But having that show light up the sky with all that crazy shit saved us. It stopped the fighting. All those HomeState guys just put down their guns and waited for the Lord. Whatever that was, I'm so thankful. Without it, we wouldn't have had a chance. We'd have been destroyed within an hour," he explains, shaking his head. "Only about half the expected Resistance fighters showed. Crucial units never made it through the western border. Planes were shot down, at least seven of them, before they ever got to us. So we didn't have the fire power, not even close. I guess it's a good thing we didn't need it."

I'll say, I think, knowing that we'd have been stuck inside the exploding mountain.

"I guess they were expecting us, despite our careful planning. There must have been spies even among us," Watson muses.

"There are always spies," says Dad.

"And counter spies," adds Sylvia, with a modest smile.

"The few of us that showed up stopped bullets," he continues, then takes a jagged breath and bows his head. "Jones was one. I had to leave her where she fell."

Watson buries his head in his hands. My dad wraps his arms around him.

"I'm not exactly sure what comes next." Watson sniffs. "Nobody is answering their messages. I can't get any of the equipment to function. No cells, no vocoms, no telejectors, not even text messages. There's nobody making any decisions, since we can't talk to each other. We're all scattered, and nothing works."

"Communications are down," explains Dad. "Not just here. All over the world. At least this is what we presume. The power of the solar wind blew all the satellites."

"Shift," says Mom quietly. "Just how big, we don't yet know."

"You're kidding," says Watson, as if he can't comprehend a world without electronic connections. "How terribly lonely." As if to prove his point, the candle flame grows big, then sputters out. We sit in darkness, listening to distant waves slap the island and to the wind shaking the trees.

"So," says Sylvia, "what are we going to do now?"

For a long, dark minute, nobody answers.

Then Dad says, "Find another candle." Darkness is nothing new to him, but he strikes a match with fanfare and illuminates our little group.

"Conserve matches," advises my mom.

"Make a plan," says Lenora.

"Begin again," adds Shriek loudly. "But first I need to go back to sleep."

+ + +

We're all up with the sunrise. This time, there's no fire in the sky, no bloody water, just an ordinary morning. The temperature isn't too hot or too cold. There haven't been any disasters in the night, no gunshots, no earthquakes. At least, not here.

We have to go find out about the rest of the world. That seems to be the plan.

Watson decides we should fill the Atro City van's tank with anything combustible—lawn-mower gas, cooking oil, lotions. Anything we can scrounge from nearby cabins. Sylvia and Watson return with half-filled containers of rancid vegetable oil, the dregs from old-fashioned lamp reservoirs, and several jars of "Essence of Youth," a skin oil promising to "take years off your face"—and now, we hope, "Can burn like gasoline!"

"Seven unopened vats of that stuff." Sylvia laughs. "What did they think? They were going to stay wrinkle-free forever?"

"That oughta be enough," Watson assures her. "So, we won't need to burn this." He holds up a quart of vodka and grins.

Hod and Tom show up. They offer to drain the *MaryLu*'s reserve tank for us. "She hasn't gone any-where for years," says Hod.

"Not much more than fumes in there anyway." Tom shrugs. "But you're welcome to it."

We protest until they assure us that they're not going out fishing until they can fix her up good and the lobsters come back.

"Whichever comes first," Hod mutters, and disappears to retrieve the gasoline.

We stand around for a while, getting ready to leave.

Shriek's down at the shore, scanning the waves for Mr. Baby Guy. "I think I see him!" she yells, dancing about, hopping up and down. And I hope she's right. Her hair whips around her freckled face, and it strikes me that she looks happy.

There's a low rumble beyond the mountain. A thunderstorm is coming in.

"Could be hail," says Tom.

"Could be worse," says Hod. "You never know what's going to fall from the sky these days."

They don't want to accompany us, even though Dad offers and there's room in the van, sort of. Maybe it's that we don't have any actual destination beyond north.

"North to where our people are," as Sylvia says. She's the one who has talked us into it. We have enough makeshift fuel in the van for nearly 700 miles, or so says Watson. That will get us close enough, Sylvia promises. She claims her sister Sally will be glad to see us and that there is a garden. It's a place we can stay for a while. We can help Sally harvest the peas and the squash. "And whoever harvests, eats." She also says we can pray to God in any way we want. "Or not, although that would be a grand shame." A little bit of the prayer Grace Ellen spoke comes back to me—*Loving God, in whom is heaven.* And I wonder if heaven could be anyplace, as long as there is love.

Maybe Hod and Tom don't want to leave because they're already home, despite the poisons and the rising sea.

"You take care, now," Tom says as fat raindrops begin to fall. They trickle down my neck, stinging gently. Hod doesn't say much, but he smiles like he means it.

We all pile into the van, and it farts into action— reeking of french fries, facial cream, and fish. Watson hunches over the wheel, full of purpose and life. We're on a new mission, and he's a mission kind of guy. I glance sideways at Lenora, amazed by how far we've come. And this seems like just the beginning.

Shriek waves wildly to Hod and Tom as they recede into the distance. She keeps waving until we can no longer see the cabin, not even the chimney. The sea, rough and gray with rain, disappears from view. The woods close up around the old dirt road, thick and dense and full of mystery. The van bounces in and out of all the ruts. As we round the corner, Shriek turns to me and smiles.

"Up north, you will see Daniel again."